HIGHLAND SEASONS

WILLA BLAIR

Laird of Lies Copyright © Linda Williams

Her Highland Deception Copyright © Linda Williams

Highland Yuletide Reunion Copyright © Linda Williams

Heart of Ice Copyright © Linda Williams

Heart of Hope Copyright © Linda Williams

Highland Fury's Legacy Copyright © Linda Williams

A Season for Longing Copyright © Linda Williams

Cover art by Dar Albert at Wicked Smart Designs

Published by Oliver-Heber Books

0 9 8 7 6 5 4 3 2 1

This book is dedicated to my fans.

When I decided to create short stories around my existing series, I didn't know what I was getting myself into. It turned out to be a lot of fun, so I hope you, too, will enjoy reconnecting with favorite characters and meeting new ones as much as I loved writing these stories about them.

ACKNOWLEDGMENTS

I've been lucky in my writing career to have worked with wonderful editors who taught me to avoid problems authors tend to be blind to in their own writing, and who often saved me from myself. My current editor at Oliver-Heber Books, Kim Ostrom, is no exception. Besides catching my mistakes, she makes valuable suggestions that make the stories you get to read even better. I truly appreciate what she does for me—and for you.

INTRODUCTION

Welcome to my first collection of short stories. Several are based on books you've read, but two are glimpses into new novels I'm writing. I enjoyed taking another look at characters in my books, expanding their stories, and creating new characters, as well.

I called this my *first* collection of short stories for a reason. I hope you'll enjoy them, too! If you do, there may soon be a second collection in the works. Please let me know by reviewing this book, or sending me a note at *willa@willablair.com*. And keep reading!

<u>*1400s - Based on the His Highland Heart Series*</u>

"Laird of Lies" - enjoy a long teaser of a new Sutherland Twins Duet novel.

"Her Highland Deception" - a look at the beginning of new His Highland Heart series novel.

"A Yuletide Reunion" - Mary Rose and Cameron Sutherland welcome her sisters and their families back to Clan Rose where not much goes as planned. This story takes place between the main story and epilogue of *HIS HIGHLAND BRIDE.*

<u>1500s - Based on the Highland Talents Series</u>

"Heart of Ice" - a prequel to my novel, *HEART OF STONE.*

"Heart of Hope" - an epilogue to my novel, *HEART OF STONE.*

"Highland Fury's Legacy" - a prequel to Jamie Lathan and Caitrin Fletcher's story in *HIGHLAND TROTH.*

"A Season of Longing" - a Yuletide epilogue to *HIGHLAND TROTH.*

LAIRD OF LIES

Cameron Sutherland's older twin brothers are mentioned in HIS HIGHLAND BRIDE (*His Highland Heart Series Book 4*), but we don't meet them there. This story is your first glimpse of a new duet based on this series.

You see Stellan and Anders Sutherland first as young twins troubled by the news that they will be wrenched apart for seven years under the clan custom of fostering sons with other clans, some far, far away.

Then as adult sons of the Sutherland laird, on missions for their father and the clan, trouble of a very different kind threatens to separate them forever.

Or will they cause a clan war to honor a vow made when they were nine?

PROLOGUE

SCOTTISH HIGHLANDS, SUMMER, 1400

"Wait for me!"

Stellan Sutherland heard his twin's faint call, but he kept going, his pace fast, his thoughts faster. He would have to break the awful news he'd just received, but how? He couldn't bear to see the hurt in Anders's eyes, and to be the one to put it there. His own distress was too recent. Too fresh and too painful for any nine-year-old to bear, but especially one like Anders who wore his heart for all to see.

If Anders got close enough, he'd know immediately what was amiss. He'd know the reason for Stellan's anger as clearly as if he'd spoken the reason aloud. Da had informed his heir, his eldest son, of his plans, with no thought to how they would affect both twins.

So Stellan kept moving, stumbling down the swale into the next glen and leaping across the rushing burn, then climbing the next hill and the next. Sutherland territory stretched farther than anyone could see, farther than he could go afoot at this pace with no food and only icy water from a burn to drink.

He hadn't planned this infuriated march. He'd simply bolted from the keep after Da had announced his plan to split them up. He sought to put an end to the canny bond they shared, the bond he feared, but they cherished. The twin bond that let them understand each other without words, and to know how the other felt without seeing so much as an expression on the other's face or the set of his shoulders.

The thought of being away from his twin for years stole Stellan's strength and he halted in the heather, panting, bent forward, hands on knees. He heard Anders shout again for him to stop. His twin was still out of sight, below the crest of the last hill, unaware Stellan had stopped and was finally waiting for him.

It was time. They were far enough from Dunrobin to give voice to their anger and grief and not have word of their indulgence in such raw emotions get back to their Da.

Anders caught up with him a few minutes later.

Stellan barely got his breath back when the look on his twin's face took it from him again.

"What has he done?"

Anders's demand jerked Stellan upright and he grimaced against the stitch in his side. "Ye dinna ken?"

"Ye are so riled, I canna pick one thing from another. So tell me."

There was no easy way to break the news he'd begun to hope Anders could pluck from him in silence. He must say the words, and the pain in his torso intensified. "Da has decreed we are to be sent to foster."

"Where? What has ye so upset?"

Anders still didn't understand. Stellan sucked down a lungful of air, then with a twist of his lips, told him, "I am to be honored to foster with Domnhall, the Lord of the Isles, for seven years. Da thinks to send ye far away, to the Norse land, surety for the treaty between we northern Scots and the Norse king."

Anders shrugged. "But we will return to Sutherland."

Stellan shook his head. "He thinks to have ye betrothed there. To someday rule the Norseland for Sutherland. Or for Scotland."

Anders's mouth fell open. Finally, he understood why Stellan was so upset.

"That canna be," he objected. "I will go with ye."

Stellen let his gaze drop to the ground. "Da will send us where he wills. We must do as he says and go."

"And ye are willing to do that?"

Anders planted his fists on his hips, displaying his growing anger that Stellan could now feel.

"I dinna believe ye," Anders continued. "Ye always have another plan, a way around our da."

"What would ye have us do?" Stellan demanded, his

earlier anguish returning. "Run away together today?" He waved a hand at the hills that marched on ahead of them, seemingly forever.

"Nay! We are lairds of Sutherland. The clan needs us, or will...someday." Anders sank to the ground and sat, his gaze confused and dismayed.

Stellan was the stronger of the two, but his heart broke for both of them. "We believed so. The laird, our grandfather, decreed it may be so. As we have always done everything else, we would rule together. But grandda is dead. Da's time has come, and he will do as he pleases."

Anders drew his *sgian dubh*. "Then we will swear a blood oath to survive and reunite to keep Sutherland safe and strong."

Stellan nodded, impressed at Anders's initiative. "Once we inherit, it will be so. And," he added, holding up his hand to stop Anders before he began to sanctify the oath with his blood, "we willna fall for any lass—or Norse princess—unless we can bring them home, so that we can fulfill our destiny to be lairds together. As is our right and our grandda's wish."

Anders scored a line in his palm. When it seeped red, he handed the blade to Stellan, who did the same. They clasped hands, mingling the blood they had once shared in the womb.

"So it will be as we have sworn this day," Stellan said. "We may be forced to part for a term of years, but we will return. Someday, we will rule Sutherland together."

"So it will be," Anders repeated, "And when the day comes that Sutherland is ours, we will keep it safe and strong—together."

———

Northern Scotland, Spring, 1412

The fire in the great hall's hearth warmed Stellan Sutherland as he waited for his twin, Anders, to shake the sleet from his hair in the keep's doorway and join him by the fire. May was late for this kind of weather, but they were far enough north, one never knew what to expect. "Come on, laggard. It'll melt, but ye willna."

Anders grimaced, gave his plaid a final shake and stepped in. "Sod off. 'Twould run down the back of my neck, as cold as the trail of a witch's finger on my skin."

"And when have ye felt the chill of a witch's finger?"

"Never. And I dinna plan to start now." Anders settled on the bench opposite his twin and signaled a passing serving maid for an ale. "'Twas a long, cold ride from Inverness. If I were eldest, I'd have been sitting here by the fire for the last fortnight, drinking and cuddling the lasses while ye froze yer arse riding home through snow and sleet."

Stellan ignored the jibe. He was older than Anders by mere minutes, a fact that meant nothing to them, but carried great weight with their father, the Sutherland laird. He could have told Anders about hunting in the same sleet storm earlier in the afternoon. And he couldn't recall the last time he'd embraced a lass, much less held one on his lap, but certainly not in the last fortnight while Anders visited Inverness on business for Sutherland. Instead he asked, "Did ye get what Da sent ye after?"

Anders nodded. "Aye, and more. I'll go tell him once I've thawed my feet."

Stellan waited, knowing he'd be present when Anders reported to their father.

Anders thanked the lass who brought him a mug of ale. She gave him a grin and a wink she also turned on Stellan, curtsied and went on her way. Anders took a long drink, following her with his gaze until she was out of sight, then lowered the cup and rolled his eyes.

Stellan knew exactly what he meant. The lasses flocked to Anders like gulls to a beached fish. His open, friendly nature made him seem more approachable than Stellan, though both were more than passably good looking. And Stellan considered himself open and friendly. Some of the time. When it suited his purposes.

They looked so much alike, anyone who didn't know them well had trouble telling them apart, a fact they'd taken advantage of many times both before and after they'd spent the years between ages nine and sixteen fostered away, Stellan with Domnhall, the Lord of the Isles and Anders sent northward, though not where their father had first threatened, across the North Sea. They'd traded off to fool their tutors of subjects one hated and the other liked. They'd fooled the cook, getting a treat, and returning as the other brother and getting another.

In the five years since they'd returned to Sutherland, they'd honored their vow to each other, neither marrying, both serving the clan much as their younger brother Cameron had done before he wed Mary Rose, traveling the countryside, gathering information for their father.

Female giggles echoed from the direction of the hallway to the kitchen. He hadn't heard that sound since Anders left for Inverness.

"I see ye havena lost your charm," he chided.

Anders sighed. "'Tis no' just me. 'Tis the two of us, together. Which is how some of them would like to try us."

Stellan laughed. On his own, the lasses were friendly, but when the twins were together, well, lasses had always been fascinated by the wee lairds, as they'd been called when they were bairns. Their fascination had grown along with them.

"Ye are welcome to them," he said. "There's none here I'd have without the lass thinking to be the next lady of the clan. I'd never be rid of them." Anders had protected Stellan by allowing him, once in a while, to pretend to be his younger twin if a lass caught his eye. During Anders's latest absence, Stellan had toyed with the idea of impersonating his brother with one of the village lasses, but decided it wasn't worth the trouble it could cause.

"Aye, that does tend to make one think twice." Anders

tossed off the last of his ale. "Very well, I'm ready. Let's go speak to Da."

They stood and made their way to the laird's solar. The door was closed, a good indication Laird Sutherland was within and working. Anders knocked.

"Come," their father's deep voice penetrated the thick, oaken door.

Stellan gave Anders an open-handed gesture to precede him. Anders opened the door and went in, Stellan following close behind.

"So, ye are back." Seated behind his work table, Laird Sutherland was a large, imposing man with glints of silver in his hair.

"Aye, father, just long enough to melt the sleet."

"And have a drink by the fire, I'll wager."

Anders colored and grinned. "I learned from the best these last five years."

Setting aside his quill, Sutherland nodded agreement, since he was well known to do the same. "So ye did." He waved them to seats. "What did ye learn?"

"There are rumors Domnhall plans another incursion, but 'tis only talk. No sign of any of his men in any numbers. The normal few ye'd expect to find anywhere in Scotland on business for the Isles. The same for any of Mar's men foolish enough to remain behind. 'Twas a wasted trip."

Sutherland nodded. "That was nay a wasted trip. Ye have brought good news. The longer Domnhall holds off, the better. No one kens why he walked away from Red Harlaw instead of finishing the fight. 'Tis something to worry us, but for now, we have other problems. If the MacKay would follow Domnhall's example, we might get through the spring and summer without more bloodshed."

Stellan turned to his twin. "No' much chance of that. In the time ye have been gone, Anders, MacKay has raided crofts on our border three times." He thought it interesting that their da wasn't concerned about Mar's left-behind men.

"So many?" Anders asked. "What about Gunn?"

"Harald Gunn sent me a missive a few days ago. He met with the MacKay recently and said with spring coming on, they're more interested in planting than stirring up trouble. I hope he kens I have reason nay to believe him."

"Likely," Anders said and nodded.

"'Tis time to see what there is to be seen toward the northwest," Sutherland continued. "Stellan, ye will take some men and ride Sutherland's borders with Gunn and MacKay."

"I'll go," Anders objected. "Ye need Stellan here."

"Ye are just back from Inverness. 'Tis time for the heir to visit our outlying crofts."

"I'll leave in the morning," Stellan said, collected Anders with a glance and left the solar.

———

MARIOTA MACKAY REMOVED THE JESSES AND LET HER HAWK Valkyrie fly free. They'd both been cooped up too long indoors, but the skies finally cleared around midday, and she loved the feel of the sun on her face. Valkyrie soared over the glen, making Mariota wish she could see through the raptor's eyes, feel the wind and weightlessness as her favorite hunter did.

She would spread her wings and never look back.

But that was a dream. And her fathers' edicts were real. Not only could she not leave MacKay land, she could not stray out of sight of the keep's imposing walls. She could not ride, or hunt with a bow, or speak her mind, or live her life the way she wished. And his men enforced his every word.

"Lasses do as they're told," her father growled the last time she reminded him she was a better shot with her bow than his men. And Valkyrie could spot and flush prey. To her, it made all the sense in the world. To him, well, she was not a son. And after the boar gored and nearly killed him five years ago, he'd never have one of his own.

She was the clan's hope for the future. Or rather, the man she'd eventually be forced to marry would be.

And if something happened to her father or her before that day came? The Lord of the Isles was ready to pounce. Or so her father believed. He'd become obsessed with two things in the last year. Finding a husband for her, and guarding MacKay against their neighbors, clan Gunn and the mighty clan Sutherland.

Valkyrie wheeled, catching Mariota's attention in time to see her stoop and dive on some prey. Good. A kill would do much to ease the frustration her winged hunter had felt at being enclosed for the last week.

She was trained to bring her kill to Mariota, a necessity if she was to be part of the clan's hunts. If the MacKay ever allowed it. Mariota watched her take wing and held up her gloved hand, a signal for the bird to return to her. As Valkyrie neared, she dropped a rabbit in front of her mistress, landed on Mariota's fist, flapped her wings to settle her balance, and stilled.

"Good lass!" Mariota told her. "A coney for the pot. Cook will be pleased with ye, even if Da is no'." She replaced the jesses, retrieved the rabbit, and made her way around the glen to the keep's gate.

"Got one, did she?" The guard, her friend Seamus, called down to her.

Mariota couldn't wave, but she held up Valkyrie's kill. "Aye. She always does. They're thick in the glen. I'm headed for the mews, then the kitchen. Can I bring ye anything? Or are ye coming down?"

"Go on about yer business, Mari. I'll visit the kitchen myself soon enough." He gave her a grin and a wave.

Mariota nodded and after returning Valkyrie to her perch in the mews, entered the kitchen with her prize.

"Been out, have ye?" The cook took the coney and laid it aside. "I shouldha kenned ye would now the weather's cleared. What will yer da say?"

"Nay a word. I stayed in Seamus's view the entire time."

"As if that lad would tell yer da any different. He fancies ye."

"Dinna ye start. Seamus is a friend and naught more."

"He'd like to be. Poor lad. 'Twill never happen."

Mariota's shoulders slumped at the reminder, however oblique, of her duty to the clan to wed a stranger.

"Ach, me and my big mouth." Cook crossed her arms over her ample chest. "Go get cleaned up, then come back. To apologize, I'll make something special for ye."

Mariota nodded and gave her a smile. "Seamus said he'd be in soon. Ye might make enough for two."

"Aye, and I will." Cook shooed her out.

Mariota headed for her chamber, eager to wash the rabbit's blood from her hands and kirtle. In the great hall, she noticed Alber sprawled in a chair by the fire, tankard in hand, and grimaced. She looked away and mounted a few stairs, hoping he was far enough in his cups not to see her. But her luck was no better this time than it ever was. He noticed her.

"Have ye killed a MacCleod, then, Mari? From the look of ye, ye did a poor job of it."

Alber's taunt rankled. She pretended she didn't hear him, but continued up the stairs without hesitation.

"Ach, nay, of course no'," he continued, louder. "Yer da willna let ye hunt, so ye canna fight for MacKay, either, can ye? Ye and yer wee bow and arrows."

His snicker was the last straw. Mariota stopped halfway

up the stairs and peered down at him. Alber was a few years her senior, big and heavily muscled, he could have grown into a good-looking man if it wasn't for the constant sneer on his face. A scar from the battle of Red Harlaw didn't help. It ran from his nose to his jaw on the left side of his face, as if his opponent had tried to blind him and missed. Alber claimed to have killed so many that day, her da thought of him as one of his best fighters. His ruthlessness made him a hero for a few weeks, until people realized he enjoyed the praise, and his tales of his prowess in the battle grew beyond anything the surviving MacKays fighting there could confirm.

When they were younger, Alber had cornered her in the stables and tried to kiss her as he shoved his hand down her chemise. For his trouble, she'd kneed him as Cook had taught her. He'd dropped to the straw, swearing. "Too good for the likes of me, are ye?" He'd spat and curled up, threatening, "Ye'll pay for this."

"No' as much as ye'll pay if I tell Da what ye just did."

Since that day, he hadn't touched her so familiarly again, but never failed to bump into her or brush her shoulder as he passed by in a crowded room. He always had something disparaging to say if he caught her alone, but so far, she'd managed not to let him corner her. She shuddered to think what he'd do, given the chance. Bad enough what he probably said about her out of her hearing. She often regretted not reporting him to her father.

Today, after her brief taste of freedom with Valkyrie,

she was in no mood to put up with Alber. "At least I brought food for the pot. What have ye done today, save sit on yer arse and drink? As ye are now, yer next opponent in battle will finish what the last started and cleave yer head from yer shoulders."

He lurched to his feet with a roar.

Mariota sniffed and continued up the stairs. He'd never follow her. If she screamed, her father would exile him, unless he chose to run him through on the spot. She went the rest of the way considering which she would prefer. Alber's curses followed her up the stairs.

———

Stellan pulled off his gloves as he entered the keep and made his way to the laird's solar. The door was open, so he didn't bother to knock. "I'm back," he announced, and moved to the hearth to chase away his chill by the fire. Days were getting longer and warmer, but by sunset, the air still carried the bite of winter.

"Ye are late. Was there trouble?" Sutherland laid aside his quill and leaned back in his chair. Numbers and notations covered the pages of the open journal on the work table before him.

"Nay. I ken ye were told MacKays are hunting Sutherland territory. We saw naught of them, though there's nay lack of places for them to hide." With some of the rawness of riding knocked off, he settled in a chair across the table from his father. "What is that?"

"The planting schedule. Barring another hard freeze, we should be able to start working the fields soon, especially those closer to the firth."

"We dinna need another lean year come harvest time. Or poachers."

"Indeed. Our stores are depleted as it is, and this time of year, we have to go farther afield to find game."

"We spotted a huge stag up north and tracked him for a few hours, but lost him in the woods. 'Tis why I'm late returning. I'll take several men tomorrow and try again."

"Have a care. The hinds will be fawning soon."

"I ken 'tis the wrong time of year to take a female. We saw none."

Anders entered then. "To ye, any time of year is the wrong time to take a female," he quipped. "Oh, were ye speaking of lasses or deer?"

"In either case, we were no' speaking to ye," Stellan replied. Anders grinned, taking no insult. Ever since they'd returned to Sutherland after fostering away, Stellan had shown no interest in taking a wife. Not until he absolutely had to. His twin understood. As young lads, they'd sworn an oath not to do so unless the lass came home with them. It didn't stop Anders from consorting with any lass who showed an interest. In the eyes of the clan, he wasn't weighed down with being the laird's heir, so like any other handsome lad, he felt free to take advantage where he could. Stellan had to be much more careful.

"So, ye saw nay sign of MacKays, either," Anders went on, clearly aware of the reason for Stellan's grim mood. "What are they up to?"

"According to the Gunn, naught," Sutherland said.

"Do ye believe him?" Stellan didn't.

"I believe only what I see or hear with my own senses," Sutherland answered.

"Or the report of yer sons," Anders prompted drily.

"Or a trusted ally, which Gunn is no'."

"So, nothing has changed," Stellan summarized, then stood. "I'm for some food and my bed."

"I've eaten," Anders told him, "but I'll join ye for an ale."

"Go on, ye two, and leave me to my work." Sutherland waved them out.

———

"Let's go riding." Mariota hooked her arm through Seamus's when she found him in the middle of the bailey the next day and turned him toward the stables. "I want to get out for a while and 'tis a fine morning."

"Yer da does no' want ye to leave the keep."

"He does no' want me to leave alone. I willna. Ye will be with me."

Seamus didn't look convinced, so Mariota stuck out

her lower lip, doing her best to look pitiable and sad. When Seamus sucked in a breath, she knew she'd won.

"We'll go," he told her, "but we must return before dark."

"Why do ye say that? We always do."

"I'm on duty tonight."

"Perfect. We willna need to hurry. If ye'll beg Cook for some food so ye can eat before we return, I'll fetch Valkyrie."

He stood firm when she tried to turn them back toward the keep. "I dinna ken if this is such a good idea."

He couldn't back out now! She could taste freedom. And her favorite mount, Epona, needed to run. Mariota hadn't been able to ride her in weeks, and the mare was used to more freedom. Chafing over her father's restrictions, Mariota thought she'd found a champion in Seamus, and feared he was wavering. "I promise we'll be back in time. With Valkyrie along, we can hunt and make the morning worthwhile. She might take another coney for the pot. Da canna complain about that."

Mariota kept her expression neutral as Seamus considered. He feared her father's wrath. Everyone did. But the gate guard would not let her ride out without an escort, and Seamus was the most amenable to her of the MacKay men.

Finally, he nodded. "Fetch her, and yer bow. I'll meet ye in the stable."

Elation filled her, but she kept it off her face. "Thank

ye." She headed for the mews to collect Valkyrie. She kept her bow there, too, so in minutes she was in the stable, instructing the lad working there to saddle Epona and Seamus's favorite mount.

By the time the horses were ready, Seamus arrived with a packet of food and two skins. He held one up. "Wine."

Mariota nodded. He knew her preference for watered wine over ale. They mounted up and Mariota settled Valkyrie on the bow-perch pommel the hawk master had carved for her. She led the way from the stable to the gate and called, "Open up."

"Ye are no' to go riding," the guard answered.

"No' alone, nay. But Seamus is with me."

"Open up," Seamus added. "We willna be gone long."

Mariota held her breath. With Seamus by her side, she hadn't expected resistance from the guard. "What did Da threaten all of ye with?" She kept her voice low enough only Seamus would hear her.

"Trust me, ye dinna wish to ken."

"Ouch."

"Pitch yer voice higher and ye'll have the right idea."

Mariota scowled at that. Surely her da wouldn't do anything so barbaric. Her expression smoothed into a smile when the gate inched open. As soon as there was enough of a gap for the horses to slip through, she kicked Epona into motion. In moments, they were free.

They rode hard across the open field outside the gate, then slowed when they entered the woods. At the first clearing, Mariota stopped and loosed Valkyrie. "Hunt," she told her. The raptor eyed her, then took to her wings and was soon lost to sight above the trees.

"She'll call if she spots something," Mariota reminded Seamus. "Until she does, let's ride."

They continued into the woods. In moments, Valkyrie's piercing call sounded above them. "That way," Seamus said, pointing.

In the next clearing, they found Valkyrie perched on her kill, a young fox. "Fox is nay good to eat, but the fur will be welcome," Mariota commented as she dismounted.

Seamus pulled his dirk, skinned the carcass, and left it for Valkyrie to enjoy. The fur he rolled and tied behind his saddle. "She didn't take long. Will she keep hunting?"

"Aye." Mari took the water skin from Epona's back as she watched Valkyrie tear strips of meat from the fox's haunch. She looked away long enough to rinse Seamus's hands and knife of blood. "She won't take much from that kill."

In moments, the bird launched skyward and they remounted.

Seamus picked up his reins. "Which way?'

"Toward the burn, I think," Mariota said. "We can wash up, refill this, and water the horses there, even if Valkyrie doesn't spot any prey."

At the burn, Seamus checked his horse's hooves. "Damn, I thought so. He's thrown a shoe."

"He's lamed?" Mariota's heart plummeted. So much for a long day away from the keep.

"Nay, but I canna ride him back to the keep without risking him. I'll have to walk him back."

At that moment, Valkyrie called. "She's spotted something. I'll go check," Mariota said.

"Dinna go far," Seamus warned. "Ye need to come with me. I canna leave ye here or yer da will have my cods, and I canna get to ye with any speed if trouble finds ye."

"I'll come back as quickly as I can." Mariota rode away, leaving Seamus to deal with his mount. Relishing her freedom to be alone, she forgot her promise to stay close by. She kept going, following Valkyrie's cries until she realized they were near the border with Sutherland, and called the bird down before they went too far.

Mariota knew she would be in trouble for coming this close to Sutherland. Seamus was well behind her, stuck waiting for her with a not-yet-lame, less one shoe horse. If he got worried and didn't wait, he'd risk his mount, or be hours walking trying to find her. Though she relished the time to herself, away from everyone, out of the keep, and away from her father's odious commands, it wasn't worth the punishment her father would mete out to Seamus if he found out—or if anything happened to her. This solitude, and feeling almost as free as Valkyrie on the wing, was an illusion.

She dismounted and walked across the clearing to where Valkyrie had landed with her kill, another bird.

Mariota would let her feast on it before they headed home. She had earned the treat. But they needed to head back soon, or Seamus would indeed start searching for her, and he'd never go with her out of the keep again.

An arrow came out of nowhere and buried itself in the ground next to Valkyrie. The hawk dropped her kill and launched herself into the air.

Mariota spun, searching for cover and for where the shot had come from. Before she could move, Alber showed himself.

"Ye are a long way from home, lass," he taunted her. "And alone. Yer lap dog, Seamus, is far from here. He can do naught to help ye, now can he? And I can do with ye what I will." He stepped closer, lips pulled back in a malicious grin. "Go on, then, scream if ye wish. Ye willna be heard. Seamus is too far away."

"I dinna need to scream," she ventured, fighting the urge to run. Alber would be on her before she could take three steps. All she could do was hold her ground and keep his attention on her. Fear made her knees weak and her heart pound, but she had a secret weapon.

She whistled, calling Valkyrie down to attack, and tilted her head toward Alber.

He laughed and continued to advance on her.

Valkyrie's attack was as swift as it was unexpected—at least for him. Before Mariota could decide to run after all, the hawk's steep dive ended with her wings flared out around his head and her claws in his neck. Instinctively, he tried to protect his throat by grabbing at her claws. She pecked his face, tearing a chunk out of his cheek. Mariota whistled her away before he could harm her.

Valkyrie launched herself skyward.

At least her bird was safe. Mariota wasn't. The look on Alber's torn face promised a painful death if he managed to get his hands on her. She was about to call Valkyrie back down when she realized how much blood flowed from his face and neck. Instead of rushing Mariota, he stumbled to his horse and clung to its saddle, no longer able to taunt or threaten her.

Valkyrie had given her time to get to her horse, and she took advantage of Alber's condition, mounted and rode for home, her hawk pacing her in the sky above her.

Before long, she found Seamus and told him what had happened. "He may be coming behind us," she warned

Frowning, Seamus said, "I'll ride double with ye. Without a rider on his back, my mount can run. We need to get back to the keep. Ye are nay safe out here."

"Da will never let me out of MacKay's walls again."

"If Alber catches ye, yer da will be the least of yer worries." He mounted up behind her. "Now let's go."

―――――

THEY REACHED THE KEEP SAFELY, BUT MARIOTA KNEW THAT wasn't the end of her peril. She still had to tell her father what happened.

"I told ye to stay inside the gates," he raged, pacing his solar after he sent men to look for the injured Alber. "Ye disobeyed me yet again. Must I lock ye in yer chamber?"

"I did as ye asked, Da. I wasna alone until Seamus's horse threw a shoe. And Valkyrie spotted prey, so I went after her. But Alber found me and threatened me. I had to call Valkyrie down to stop him from...hurting me. Maybe even killing me." Probably. If he'd violated her, he couldn't have let her live to tell the tale. But Mariota didn't think her da was prepared to hear that from her.

His frown and the way his jaw clenched gave her hope he understood what she hadn't said. Alber would not get out of this unpunished, either.

"If ye had stayed in the keep as ye ought, this wouldna have happened. Seamus will be punished for aiding ye."

"Ye canna do that, Da. Blame me if ye must. I convinced Seamus to ride with me. But dinna blame me for what happened to Alber. He did no' have to follow. Or to threaten me. He tried to kill Valkyrie first, but his arrow missed. He got nay more than he deserved."

"And so shall ye. Get ye to yer chamber. I'll deal with ye after the men return."

Mariota realized she'd get nowhere arguing with her father. Meekly, she nodded and did as he ordered.

An hour later, he called her back. His men had found Alber unconscious, blood still seeping from the wounds on his neck and face.

"He does no' deserve to die," her father raged once he

gave her the news. "Certainly no' in this way! Killed by yer damn hawk? If the lads had no' found him when they did, he would be dead, and MacKay would be without one of its best fighters. Ye, lass, are of an age to cause more such trouble. There are rough men here. More since Domnhall sent troops to fight Mar. I will see ye married. And soon."

Mariota gasped. This was to be her punishment? Her father cared less for her than for the man who'd tried to ruin his daughter—his heir—and instead of punishing him, was determined to marry her off? To whom? Surely not Alber! The very idea made cold sweat trickle down her spine.

"And no' to that lad Seamus. He may be yer friend and protector, but marriage to him does naught for MacKay. We need an alliance. And I know just where to seek one."

"Nay, da. I dinna wish to marry. No' Seamus, nay any other MacKay, and certainly no' with a stranger."

"Ye ken yer place, daughter. Ye will do yer duty for the clan."

"Ye are punishing me for Alber's actions."

"Perhaps I am, but for yers as well. Ye must learn what ye do has consequences. In this case, ye nearly cost a man's life."

"He brought that on himself when he attacked me." If nothing else, she had to make her father understand how dangerous Alber was to her.

"I will no' argue with ye, daughter. Leave me now, or there will be even more consequences."

He'd confine her to her chamber, or deny her Valkyrie, or something else she couldn't bear. With gaze downcast, she nodded, turned, and left the solar. She would go to her chamber, but not for any longer than necessary. She needed time to gather her things, and to find a way to get out of the keep's walls without being seen. Running away was dangerous, even foolish, she knew, but she knew her father. He'd do what he'd promised and marry her off, probably to some old laird of an enemy clan, for the sake of one of his damned alliances. She couldn't bear the thought. She'd rather live on her own in a hut in the woods. With Valkyrie to help her hunt, she'd never starve. But first she had to free Valkyrie and get away.

Then she'd deal with the rest of her life.

———

STELLAN RAISED A HAND, ORDERING THE HUNTING PARTY TO halt just below the next rise. They'd tracked the huge stag for three days, headed north toward MacKay. Stellan knew they were still on Sutherland territory, but they couldn't go much farther. If they didn't get lucky soon, the stag would escape them.

Their horses nickered softly, but no one spoke. Stellan dismounted, crept to the hill's crest and stretched out on the ground to peer over it. The big stag had disappeared over the hill and into the thicker woods just beyond a wee glen that marked the boundary. Into MacKay territory.

His friend Tormund crept up and stretched out beside him. "See him?"

"Nay, and we're at our border with MacKay. If he doesna wander back this way, we willna be able to keep after him."

"Bollocks. We've been chasing that bastard for days. We canna lose him to the MacKays."

"We can and we will. He's crossed the border." Stellan raised a hand to forestall Tormund's objection. "Likely he wanders back and forth at will. If we wait, we'll see him on this side again."

Tormund eyed the sun's position low in the south-western sky, snorted and pushed up onto his knees. "Unless the MacKays get him first. 'Tis done then. I'm for making camp. Let's let him live another day."

Stellan nodded and got to his feet. As he did, the stag meandered out of the trees and back across the glen's small clearing well ahead of them, nibbling at green shoots as he went. "He does no' bloody care that he's run us all over the countryside. Look at him."

Tormund crossed his arms over his massive chest. "He kens we're here."

"Aye. And if we go at him, he'll duck back into those trees on the MacKay side."

A hawk circled over the stag and emitted a piercing cry.

The stag's head came up and he froze.

"He's too big for the likes of ye," Tormund muttered, clearly addressing the raptor.

Before Stellan could answer, the stag bolted—straight for them.

"What the hell?" Tormund raised his bow, but Stellan put a hand on his arm.

"Wait till he's well on our side. Wait." Stellan's gaze swept the area between their hilltop and the stag, looking for the stone marker he knew was in the glen. He spotted it as the stag crossed into Sutherland and began to run uphill. "Give him another...wait...now!"

Tormund loosed his arrow and struck the stag in the throat.

It went down, stumbling, onto its foreleg knees, and rested there, wheezing, as blood began to soak its shoulder.

Stellan nocked an arrow and loosed it, finishing the beast. "I didna want to see him suffer," he said, waving at the others to bring the horses up.

Tormund nodded and they started down the hill. An arrow whizzed by and buried itself in the ground behind them. They ducked and scrambled for the cover of a fallen tree trunk.

"Sodding Sutherland thieves!" The angry call came from MacKay land. Another arrow followed it.

"Stay back," Stellan warned his men, then peered over the trunk and faced toward the buck. "We've stolen noth-ing," he called out.

"The buck was on MacKay land. 'Tis ours!"

"We've chased that buck over half of Sutherland. It

crossed into MacKay and back out again before we killed it. Ye have nay claim."

The rumble of deep male voices came to them, none clear, until one rose above the others to object, "That blasted bird spooked it and it ran. We'd have it but for the hawk."

"Ye did no' ken the buck was even there until the hawk screamed a warning," another said.

The voices dropped, but continued wrangling. Stellan sat back against the tree trunk and looked aside to where Tormund was doing the same. They traded a look and shrugged.

"Think we can retrieve it?" Tormund's grin gave away the sarcasm in his question.

"Go right ahead," Stellan told him. "It ye want yer arse shot full of arrows while ye try to pull it up here."

"Guess we'll have to wait until they give up and leave."

"Aye. If they do. MacKays are no' kenned for being reasonable."

The arguing continued in the MacKay camp with occasional forays to yell insults at the Sutherlands. With dark encroaching, the MacKays lit a campfire visible through the trees on their side.

Tormund groaned when the glow of the fire became visible. "Damn MacKays. 'Tis our buck."

"They'll be watching it from under the cover of those trees. Let's make a show of withdrawing."

Tormund grinned and nodded. "Anders is going to be sorry he missed this."

Stellan stayed down but moved uphill as he ordered his men back over the hilltop. He didn't bother to lower his voice, wanting the MacKays to hear him.

On the other side of the hilltop, out of earshot of the rival clansmen, he told his men, "Let them drink themselves *pished*, then we'll haul the buck over the hill and be gone before the sun comes up. Tormund and Finlay, ye'll take first watch. Wake me when they get quiet."

Two hours later, Stellan and four men picked up the buck and brought it back over the hill—a Sutherland victory his da would appreciate. The only life lost was the buck's.

———

FINDING A WAY TO ESCAPE MACKAY WAS TAKING MARIOTA longer than she'd hoped it would. She couldn't free Valkyrie, claim a horse, and get all three out of the keep, herself included, without garnering too much notice. Her father had laid down the law with the guards. Under no circumstances was she to leave the keep. Not alone and not with anyone else, especially Seamus, who had been permanently relegated to the nighttime watch. She was sorry for him, but her da could have done worse.

Alber had been under the care of the healer. Despite all the blood Mariota had seen and her da's claim that he'd been found near death, his injuries were not as serious as she'd imagined. In Valkyrie's favor, he'd never look the same again, not that Mariota thought he'd been an attractive man to start with. Her hawk's claw marks would scar his neck. The chunks the raptor had torn out of his face would heal, but would leave unsightly pits. Bruises, though those would fade, further detracted from his appearance. So she'd been told. She hadn't been foolish enough to get anywhere near his chamber.

He was under no such compunction. Mariota found him waiting outside her chamber door after the evening meal the day after he was brought back to the keep.

"Alber! What are ye doing here?" She shouted at him, hoping someone would hear and come to her aid.

"I've come to finish the business between us. Yer bird did this to me," he said and lifted a hand to his face, open wounds seeping still.

Hadn't the healer bandaged them? Or had he torn off the coverings to try to frighten her with his grotesque appearance.

"She protected me."

"She's no' here now." He moved more quickly than she thought him capable of, grabbed her arm and forced her against the wall, his other hand splayed over her face, fingers gripping the sides of her head in a punishing show of strength. "Ye are mine and ye owe me. I'll make ye hurt as yer damn bird hurt me."

Mariota tried to scream, but he flattened his palm

against her nose and mouth, denying her breath. He meant to kill her, and she was on her own. But she'd beaten him before, once by herself and once with Valkyrie's help. She'd do it again.

She tried to twist away, but it was a ruse. He fell for it, stepping wide to contain her as she writhed. With no mercy, she kneed him between the legs. She couldn't believe he fell for the same maneuver again. She went into her chamber and bolted the door as his howl echoed down the hallway. She suspected it could be heard in the great hall. In moments, running footsteps proved her right.

Two MacKay men reached her door as she opened it, followed by two more and several women.

"He attacked me again," she said. "I stopped him."

The women took in Alber lying on the floor, hands between his legs cupping himself, tears mixing with the blood seeping from his face from his fall, and laughed. "Ye got him good, lass."

"Get him away from me. Please. Lock him in his chamber and tell my da what he did."

"We'll take care of him," one of the men said, nodded to the others and they dragged Alber down the hall toward the stairs. In moments, she heard the hard thump, thump, thump that told her they dragged him *down* them, too. It seemed she wasn't the only one who disliked him. But where were they taking him? To her da?

"Did he hurt ye?" One of the older women asked in a sympathetic tone, reaching out to touch her arm.

"He tried," Mariota told her and the others who remained. "I didna let him."

"Ye are a braw lass," one of the others said.

"Thank ye, but I dinna think he's entirely recovered from the injuries he got from attacking me yesterday." She shrugged and winced. "I'd like to go rest now."

With understanding nods, they left her in her chamber. There, she gave in to a fit of shakes, angry tears stinging the corners of her eyes. She was out of time. Once Alber was well, no matter what her father might do, he'd come after her.

A knock on her door startled her. Not Alber again, please! Nay, he wouldn't knock. "Who is it?"

"Yer da sent me to guard yer door, lass." She recognized the voice of one of the men who'd carried off Alber. So, she was confined to her chamber after all. Da might think it was for her safety, but she knew better. Alber would find her alone eventually. Or her da would find her a husband whether she liked it or not.

Left with no alternative, she waited until midnight, made a rope out of bedsheets and with her few belongings wrapped in a spare plaid tied on her back, she climbed out of her window and down to the bailey. The night was quiet and the guards' attention was outside the walls, not inside, so she was able to sneak to the mews and free Valkyrie. The stable tempted her, but she knew she'd never get out with her horse. Keeping to the shadows, she turned for the postern gate, and once through it, made her way on foot to the village, staying under the trees and out of sight of the guards on the keep's walls. She knew the value of a horse to each villager, and she hated to do it, but she was desperate. She saddled and stole one she knew, vowing to return it as soon as she could, led it quietly away from the village and the MacKay keep before mounting it, and rode into the night.

———

STELLAN AND HIS MEN CONTINUED TO HUNT, MAKING THEIR way slowly back toward the keep with the buck tied over the back of one of the horses. They stopped once to field dress the buck when he was certain they were far enough into Sutherland territory the MacKays wouldn't dare follow. Hoisting it up by its hind legs and a rope slung over a tree branch, they cut its throat and drained the last of its blood, gutted it and left the entrails for the local predators. Then they moved away and found a spot near a burn to get some sleep before continuing their journey home.

Stellan woke to a guard's hand on his shoulder, early sunlight in his eyes, and the sound of a horse moving nearby rustling in the undergrowth beyond their camp, headed their way. With no fire to warn of their presence, he expected the rider would be on them in moments. He stood and toed two more men awake. "Someone's coming," he told them quietly.

They nodded, got up, and soundlessly reached for weapons.

Stellan couldn't have been more surprised when he saw a lass on horseback with a hawk in jesses gripping her fist stumble on their camp. Her long hair tumbled around her shoulders, amber threads among the rich brown catching the eastern glow. She looked half asleep and barely aware enough to avoid getting knocked off her horse by tree branches as she rode.

"Lass," he said softly as he grasped the horse's bridle to keep her from jerking awake and galloping away. They were covered in deer blood and would frighten her when she noticed it.

"What? Ach! Who are ye? Let me go."

"I'll let ye go when ye are awake enough to ride safely. I'm Stellan. Who are ye?"

She studied him, her moss-green eyes widening as she took in his and his men's bloody clothes.

No amount of dunking in a shallow burn would remove all of it, though they'd tried.

"Did ye kill the men following me?"

Stellan straightened, alert to more trouble. "Men are following ye? Who?"

"MacKays." She looked around as if looking for the men—or for a way out.

Tormund came up and gave her a nod before turning to Stellan. "Likely 'tis why that lot were so close to our border last night, aye? Searching for her and found our buck."

Stellan agreed. If the men they'd left behind were the only MacKay patrol, they were probably hung over this morning and the Sutherlands were safe. But he doubted they'd been sent out alone. Still, the lass needed assurances. "We havena killed anyone but a buck, lass, and ye are safe with us. Now, who are ye?"

"Mariota. I'm...lost, I think. Can ye help me? I wasna safe where I came from."

"'Tis lucky ye found us. We're headed home to Sutherland," he said and nodded toward the buck's body tied over one of the horses. "Come with us and we'll see ye taken care of. But first, get down. We're about to break our fast. Ye must be hungry."

Once she was off her horse, he realized she was hurt, scratched, limping, and couldn't continue on her own.

"I need to free Valkyrie to hunt," she told him. "I've kept her hooded to keep her quiet since I left home."

"Will she return to ye?" Could the lass be lying? Had she stolen a valuable bird?

"Of course. I trained her well." Mariota removed the jesses and tossed the bird into the air.

To Stellen's consternation, it flew off, but before long, it returned, a vole clutched in its claws, dropped the prey near the lass, and at her signal, settled on the ground to tear at it. He couldn't help but be impressed.

Over their own meal, Mariota told him of how she'd been attacked three times, and how Valkyrie saved her the second time after her attacker narrowly missed killing the raptor. Stellan knew he was taking a dangerous step—MacKay could say he stole the lass and ruined her—but her harrowing tale gained his sympathy and his cooperation. Her tale was too real to ignore, and her bravery impressed him. She'd fought off the last attack in her own hall.

Mariota was like no lass he'd ever met. She intrigued him, and he vowed to find out more about her. Before they headed south, he gave her spare clothes and a man's bonnet to hide her hair in case they were unlucky enough to happen near a MacKay patrol foolish enough to be looking for her on Sutherland territory.

The trip back to Dunrobin went much faster than the trip out because they weren't meandering around the countryside, on the trail of the huge buck. They rode straight through to the Sutherland keep on the Moray firth.

Stellan introduced Mariota to the clan steward to settle her in a chamber, her hawk in the mews, and to get her whatever she needed. By the time Stellan delivered the buck to the kitchen, he was tired, again covered in blood, and ready for a hot bath, but first he had to explain Mariota to the laird. He enlisted Cook's help. Rather than having hot water hauled up to his chamber, he used the tub in the screened-off nook off the kitchen, stripped and slid in with a satisfied groan. Cook had left soap and bath sheets. He was content to stay until the water cooled, but the laird awaited. So did Mariota.

Anders shouted his name, waking him from the near doze brought on by warm comfort and exhaustion. "Ah, there ye are. So Cook is stewing ye for our supper?"

"No' likely," Stellan answered, stood and let the water run down his torso before grabbing the top bath sheet from the stack and wrapping it around his waist. "What's so urgent ye have to come find me here?" He stepped out of the tub and frowned at his twin.

"I heard ye picked up a stray. And Da wants us."

"Now, of course." He grabbed the next towel and rubbed his hair as dry as he could. "I have to dress."

"Best hurry, then. I'll go stall him."

Anders left and Stellan headed for his chamber, making a point to ignore the admiring glances the kitchen wenches and other clan womenfolk sent his way. Why hadn't he sent for clean clothes before he got in the damned tub? In his chamber, he dressed quickly, then hurried to the laird's solar. Anders and their father were standing at the work table, studying a map.

"Ye needed to see us?" Stellan moved toward them.

"Are ye surprised? What the hell were ye thinking?"

"That the lass was lost, exhausted, and needed help. She's a MacKay."

"I'm well aware. Mariota."

"Aye." A shiver ran down Stellan's back. What did his da know?

"I received a missive from the MacKay. The second on the subject actually, two days ago."

"What subject?"

Anders moved around the table to stand with his twin.

Sutherland gestured them to chairs. "His daughter, Mariota, is of marriageable age."

Stellan exchanged a shocked glance with Anders. This was trouble, indeed. Did she leave because she was to be wed rather than the story she told about being attacked?

"Last fall," their father continued, "he proposed an alliance when ye both were away. I posed it to Cameron. Ye ken he looked in another direction for a wife."

"Mary Rose, aye." According to the missives Stellan had read, it was a love match.

"MacKay never actually designated which of ye lads he would like to see wed to his daughter. Now, something has happened to give her marriage some urgency and he writes that he wants a Sutherland to come to MacKay to meet her. And for the betrothal."

"He's jesting. Or ye are." Anders frowned. "When did ye say ye received his missive?"

"Two days past. She found ye in Sutherland territory today, so her da sent the missive before she ran off."

"Or escaped, by her telling," Stellan reminded him. "And she's fallen right into our hands."

"How many men would have to go with us to ensure he didn't kill us out of hand once we crossed into MacKay territory?" Anders frowned at their father.

Stellan agreed. It was madness to do what the MacKay asked.

"None. He guarantees safe passage."

"He doesna ken we have her," Anders stated.

"Nay, and by now, he's probably quite concerned about our response since he canna produce her."

"But we can."

Anders's speculative look, eyebrows raised, told Stellan he was thinking—hard. "Why Sutherland and no' one of his other allies. Sinclair or MacLeod?" Stellan frowned. "He must be nervous about Domnhall."

"I would be if I were he," Sutherland said. He shrugged, then studied both twins and seemed to come to a decision. "I will notify him that she's made her way here. Since he will doubt she has remained untouched, I must agree to the betrothal. If his response is still favorable, she must return home until the wedding."

Stellan shook his head. "Da, ye canna. She fled because she feared a clansman."

"If she's betrothed to Sutherland, do ye think her da will allow her to be harmed?"

"We canna be certain..."

"Anders, ye will go—with an escort. Stellan," he added, holding up a hand as both he and Anders opened their mouths to object, "I have other plans for ye."

The twins exchanged frowns.

"Da—"

"I'll hear nay more about this for today. I have a letter to write. Both of ye, out." He gestured at the door.

Stellan and Anders took their accustomed seats by the great hall's hearth, and after a lass brought them ale, Stellan tipped his mug. "Cheers, brother. What do ye think of our lass?"

Anders choked on the mouthful of ale he'd just taken in and sprayed it toward the fire, which leapt when the alcohol hit it. "Yer lass, ye mean," he said when he could breathe.

"Da wants ye to return her to MacKay. What do ye think he means, save that he's expecting ye will wed her?"

Anders shook his head. "He may think so, but ye found her. Ye seem to like her. Ye should be the one to travel with her, to meet her da, even to marry the lass."

"There's one problem with that," Stellan said, staring into the fire.

Anders flinched. "Aye, she's her father's heir. Her husband must rule MacKay with her. And ye are da's heir, so he expects ye will rule here after him. I'm the expendable one."

"Nay to me. Nay to the vow we made."

Anders nodded, then grinned. "Do we switch? Ye go as me to spend more time with her, and I stay as ye?"

"And when we are discovered?" Stellan couldn't imagine the outcry that would cause.

Anders shook his head. "As long as ye manage to

control yerself and dinna ruin the lass so ye are forced to marry her, ye can leave her there, and come home."

"Aren't ye forgetting da said they probably think that has already happened? Da can decide to betroth ye to her. Me. One of us!" Stellan tossed off the rest of his ale, tempted to hurl the cup into the fire for the satisfaction of watching it shatter. They'd known a day would come when the Sutherland would try to settle wives on them. Mariota had unwittingly made that day today. "God's bones, she's the one lass I can never have. Da willna accept her for me. And I swore with ye when we thought ye would be sent to the Norse land forever that we wouldna marry any lass we couldna bring home."

"We were nine," Anders replied, his tone dry.

"We were wiser than our years." He clenched the fist holding the cup. "Ye dinna want her, but I've seen enough to ken I might."

"Then ye had best go with her so ye can find out if she's worth the battle the two of ye will start."

HER HIGHLAND DECEPTION

The story of Calum Brodie and Ella Munro Ross begins in HIS HIGHLAND HEART *(His Highland Heart Series Book 2). Calum falls in love with Ella at first glance. But after escaping a forced marriage, she has no interest in men and spurns his every advance.*

In HIS HIGHLAND LOVE *(His Highland Heart Series Book 3), Calum is blinded during the battle at Red Harlaw and carried home to be cared for.*

In this story, written to be included in a new novel in the His Highland Heart series, Ella wants to help him. Fearful that he will be forever a burden and embarrassed by the intimate care he needs, Calum rejects her help.

Stung but determined, she disguises her voice and her scent and becomes "Janet", the healer's assistant. What will she do when Calum finds out?

JULY 24, 1411 - A FIELD NEAR HARLAW, FIFTEEN MILES WEST OF ABERDEEN, SCOTLAND

Calum Brodie stood with his chief, Iain Brodie, on the ridge overlooking the empty field outside the village of Harlaw. "We're close enough to Aberdeen, like as no' there will be townsfolk come to watch the battle soon," he said.

Iain nodded toward Mar's troops massed on the other side of the field, a mix of knights in mail on horseback, men with spears and halberds, and men on foot, dressed in rough clothing, carrying short swords, pikes, pitchforks, whatever weapons they had to hand. Most looked little different from many in Domnhall's army. "That lot are merchants and farmers, no' fighters. If we're lucky, they'll decide to blend in with the townsfolk and disappear."

"We can hope so."

"Aye, well, hope never won a battle, did it?"

Calum turned to face the men arrayed behind the

Brodie laird. They were ready, weapons sharp and faces grim. But their eyes gave away their eagerness for the battle to begin. This day, they fought for Domnhall of Islay, the Lord of the Isles, against the Regent of Scotland, the Earl of Mar, both of whom claimed the same Ross territory. "Domnhall had best give the signal soon," he said to Iain.

Iain pulled his claymore from the sheath on his back.

The heavy longsword flashed, blinding Calum for a moment with the sun's reflection. Iain took great care with his weapons, much as he did with his clan, and had sharpened and polished it to shine. He wanted an enemy to see death coming for him.

"Let's show him we're ready, aye?" Iain looked over his clansmen and raised his voice, thrusting his claymore skyward. "Are ye here to watch or to fight?"

"Fight, fight, fight," rang out and echoed back from the nearby hills.

"For Brodie!" Iain called out when the noise died down and raised his blade again.

In answer, the Brodie oath, "Unite!" rang out and filled the field. The men broke into raucous cheers as other clans allied with them called out their war cries in turn. Calum, heart racing, grinned at Iain. He was a master at rousing his men.

Kenneth Brodie, Iain's second-in-command, joined them. "T'will be a good day," he said. "The fog has lifted. We can see every man they have and how they move."

A cold chill ran down Calum's back.

"Dinna say that," Iain scolded. "Lest ye curse us."

Kenneth frowned, then nodded. "Ye have the right of it. I take it back," he added and crossed himself.

Despite Kenneth's words, Calum studied the opposing force. Knights on horseback, mail glinting in the summer sunlight, were easiest to see, though Mar had positioned them toward the rear of his massed spearmen. Domnhall's army vastly outnumbered Mar's, but Mar's knights could make up for their lack of numbers. Men on horseback moved faster. React faster. Their steeds' hooves and teeth could be as deadly as the steel their riders carried. Domnhall's men would have to take them down as early in the battle as possible.

Calum would be glad when this fight was over. It should settle control of Ross territory that had been under dispute for years. Even though he'd met Ella because of it, he'd be glad to see it done.

Ella. Nay, he couldn't think of the lass today. He must concentrate on staying alive, returning to her so that he could, someday, win her heart. No matter how he tried, she gave him no encouragement, but he wouldn't stop. He understood what she'd been through when stolen by Ross warriors and forced into a marriage she didn't want. She needed to be in command of her own destiny. But he was determined that destiny would include him.

First, he had to stay alive.

Finally, the order came. A cry went up, immediately

joined by a host of others. Roars and thundering hooves filled the air as the two sides rushed at each other, cavalry pushing to the fore. Calum fought alongside Kenneth, both staying near Iain, charged with protecting their laird.

In moments, Calum lost himself in the rage of battle, his senses aware of everything around him. Arms lifting, blades flashing in the summer sun, cries of battle and screams of agony, the clash and clang of weapons and shields, thunder of horses' hooves, neighs and equine screams of distress, the reek of sweat, blood and piss. It all blended into a single awareness, himself at the center, Iain and Kenneth at his sides. He had no recognition of time passing. He measured the progress they made by the number of foes surrounding them. The battle eddied and swirled as they fought off knights and farmers with the same ferocity.

A sudden lull in the numbers of men coming at them gave Calum a moment to catch his breath, chest heaving. Then he felt Iain move behind him and shout a warning. They'd let down their guard!

Only when Calum turned to defend Iain, his gaze sweeping around them, did he become aware of another danger. Iain and Kenneth fought Iain's attacker, but another loomed at Calum's side. Too close. He had only a moment to think that if they lost Iain because of it, he'd rather die here than live with the shame. He raised his sword to block the blow aimed at separating his head from his shoulders. Blades crashed and sparked, the clang loud enough to make his ears ring. Something hit his head and the side of his face. He had only a moment to regret that he would never get the chance to wed Ella before everything around him went black.

———

Calum woke to pain, as if hands spanned his head, squeezing until his skull cracked. Thought was too heavy to reach the surface unless it leaked through his skull with blood and brains. A strange whistling filled his ears. Horror made his belly roil and he heard a low groan. His? He couldn't move, couldn't even open his eyes. Something cool dripped onto his lips and into his mouth. He swallowed and went away, back into the blackness.

The next time he woke, the pain in his head had spread to his eye, sharp and piercing. Had he been stabbed in the eye? He managed to lift one hand, intending to pull out the blade, but cool fingers forced his hand back to his side and a feminine voice said something he couldn't comprehend. Male voices rumbled in the background, blurred and indistinct below the whistling. Nothing made sense, so Calum let the world go away again.

This time, he came awake with the determination to find out what had happened to him.

"Ah, Calum, good morrow."

He knew that voice. He loved that voice. Ella! What was she doing on the battlefield? He struggled to open his eyes, to sit up, to find his sword and protect her, but a hand on his chest held him down.

"Dinna move, laddie," a firm, older, female voice commanded. Not Ella. Where had she gone?

"Ella..." He tried to open his eyes, but couldn't.

"Here, Calum." Soft fingers wrapped around his and he relaxed. The women would not be on the battlefield unless the fighting was over and they had won. When had they followed Iain's men from Brodie? Calum thought Iain had left them safe within its walls, hand-picked men remaining to defend them.

"Iain?" He croaked out the name, dreading the news he might receive. "Kenneth?"

"Hale and nearby," the older voice replied.

He recognized the clan's healer's voice.

"What happened? Why canna I see? Who is making that whistling sound?"

"Ye were wounded, lad, as ye ken."

Her tone was matter-of-fact. Calm. Yet Ella's cool fingers tensed on his hand.

"How bad?"

"A crack to yer heid, and ye can be glad 'tis so hard, ye yet live. But the sword that did it shattered. Ye had a sliver of steel in yer eye. 'Tis gone now."

Her comment stopped him from trying to lift a hand to his face yet again.

"Yer eyes are covered and bandaged round yer heid. Ye must rest and heal if ye hope to see again out of that eye."

"How long?"

"Another sennight, I think. Or a wee more. I'll judge as ye go," she told him. "Ella, go fetch some broth from the kitchen. Our lad is awake enough to drink and it will help him heal."

Ella squeezed his hand and the swish of fabric told Calum she'd done as the healer asked.

"Ella will care for ye, and see to yer needs," the woman continued, "until ye can do for yerself. Ye must stay abed and keep yer head still."

Calum didn't like the sound of that. "Nay," he said, forcing the word between dry lips. "Nay Ella. I'll no' abide her seeing me like this. One of the lads can attend to me."

"If that is what ye wish." Her voice communicated disappointment. "And here I thought ye pined for her. Months ago, ye confided in me that ye wished for her to be yers. Now that ye need her, ye dinna want her?"

"I do wish it," Calum insisted once the healer's complaint ran down. "But nay like this. Send Ella away, back to Brodie. She doesna belong here."

"Lad, we are at Brodie. Ye are in yer own bed. Where did ye think..."

Shock turned his blood to ice, then he warmed again, safe. "I thought...the battlefield. Outside Aberdeen. How did I get home?"

"In a cart. Fortune smiled on ye, and ye made the journey safe in Hypnos' arms, unaware of yer pain. Ye came to me only a pair of days after ye took yer wounds.

Iain made certain ye were cared for until ye arrived. Ye've had little fever, and if ye do as I say, ye'll have nay more. But ye must do as I say. To save yer sight, ye canna move yer head overmuch. Do ye ken?"

"How have...how will I..." Suddenly he didn't want to know what had gone before, while he slept.

"I'll have someone see to ye, and check on ye myself, often. Dinna fash, lad. All will be well."

Calum heard her words but they faded into a well of sound, as if she moved far away from him, under the whistling instead of in front of it. He wanted to reach for her, to pull her back, but she'd said not to stir. So instead, he faded away, too.

———

"Dinna go in," the healer, who waited for Ella outside Calum's door, told her. "He sleeps again and we must speak." She gestured to move away, down the hall.

Ella frowned at her, then set the heavy tray she carried on the hallway floor as the woman closed the door to Calum's chamber. "About what?"

The older woman took her arm and led her toward the stairs she'd just climbed. "Now that he's awake, he doesna want ye to care for him, to see him..." She paused and frowned at the door. "The way he is now."

"But..."

"Ye are no' married and he has intimate needs unfit for a lass no' his wife or servant."

"I'm well aware." Ella canted her head, wondering if the healer had forgotten who'd taken care of those needs since he'd been brought home. Or if Calum was too insensible to recall that she'd been stolen from Munro and married to a Ross against her will. She was well schooled about men's bodies. "I dinna care about that. I care about him."

"I ken ye do, lass. Ye havena left his side since he was carried in and put into his bed. 'Tis glad I am to ken ye return his affection. But now he's awake and uncomfortable with ye tending him..." She shrugged. "I'll do as he asked and find a lad or a serving wench."

"Nay!"

"What would ye have me do, lass? He refuses yer care. I canna spend all my time with him. Others need my skills, too."

"Aye, I ken it." Ella crossed her arms and leaned against the wall at her back, thinking. "What if he doesna ken 'tis I?"

"What do ye mean, lass? He kens ye well."

"I can change my voice, my gait, my touch, as I did when I was a lass playing with the other bairns at 'warriors and maids'." She cleared her throat and lowered her voice's pitch. "Do ye think he'd ken this voice?" She raised it to a high, clear, child's tone. "Or this?"

The healer smiled. "The lower pitch will serve ye

better, especially if ye speak softly. Dinna be as gentle with him as ye have in the past. 'Twould help if yer hands were rougher."

"'Tis easily done. Annie has set the maids to making soap. If I help them, the lye will do what's needful, and quickly." The Brodie lady would welcome another pair of hands to help with the onerous chore.

"Go on with ye, then. Ah, wait a wee. What shall I call ye?"

"Janet. Call me Janet. 'Tis a common enough name for a lass."

"Soap," the healer muttered. She closed her eyes and sniffed. "Does he ken yer scent?"

"I...perhaps. I kenned my husband's and hated it."

"Of course ye did. He was forced on ye. Ye had every reason to hate him." She rested her chin on her hand for a moment. "We must find something that will give ye—give Janet—a scent all her own. An herb or spice rubbed into yer clothes might serve. Something pleasant or something strong?"

"I dinna want him to be drawn to Janet's scent."

The healer grinned as Ella pushed off from the wall with her elbows. "I'll make certain of that."

———

15 AUGUST, 1411

Ella led Calum along the path through the nearly

empty bailey, gravel crunching under their boots. With most of the keep's residents either inside preparing the great hall for the Marymas feast or out of the keep taking part in family celebrations or hunting, the healer had agreed it would be quiet enough there if she didn't take him far and was careful. To her, the brilliant afternoon sunshine seemed an odd counterpoint to the darkness Calum had lived in for three sennights. Though he couldn't see it, she hoped the change in his surroundings and the fresh air would help speed his recovery.

"We're near the stables," he suddenly remarked, lifting his head in its direction. "I smell horses."

Startled, Ella nodded, then remembered to speak in Janet's low, clipped tones. Calum had suffered ringing in his ears since the battle. Just before they came outside, the healer had removed the packing from them that muffled sound, worrying Ella. She had relied on it to help alter her voice, but the healer had insisted it come out. "Aye, we are. What else do ye smell?" She hoped the onions in her pocket continued to mask her own scent. She'd rubbed their juice on her hands and even chewed on wild onion stems to keep her own hidden behind something unpleasant. Likely he'd gotten used to the onion scent around her and knew she wasn't asking about herself. She hoped by the time they ended this deception she would not be permanently stained with the odor.

"Something acrid...woodsmoke," Calum told her. "The blacksmith's forge."

"We're approaching it. How did ye ken?" The forge was still, lacking on this feast day the clang of the smith's hammer on his anvil. The healer had agreed to this foray because the bailey would be more quiet than usual. She wanted to know if Calum's hearing had improved.

Calum remained silent for a few moments as they walked farther. "My life depends on what I notice around me," he told her. "The iron has a tang that I taste as well as smell...and I felt the heat from the banked forge as we neared it."

"I did no'," she told him. What else did he notice that she failed to discern?

"I've lived in this keep most of my life," he added. "I can find my way around this bailey blindfold..." He stopped suddenly, stiffened and sucked in a breath.

Ella laid her free hand on her heart, pity for him welling up at his words. He would hear it in her voice, so she took a breath and tried encouragement. "Aye, ye can, Calum, very well. Yer senses are undimmed by yer time indoors."

"I am...I was a Brodie scout," he said, turning his face aside as though staring off into space while recalling the battle that had made him an invalid these past weeks. "One of the best. What am I, if I can no' longer be what I was?"

Ella wanted to hold him, to reassure him, but knew she had no answer to give him. If he wasn't acting out in frustration over his enforced blindness, he fretted over his future, his place in the clan. She reached for something to lighten his mood. "Ye need no' think to become a bard—ye dinna have the voice for it," she told him in a teasing tone. As soon as she said the words, she regretted them. Would Calum realize Janet had never seen him drunk and singing drinking songs with other men, but Ella had?

His brow furrowed, telling her she had his attention. Calum's lips tightened, then twisted, one side quirking up in a hard fought attempt at a smile.

Relieved he didn't seem to have made the connection, Ella couldn't help smiling back. If his sense of humor was returning, he truly was getting better.

Then his hands curled into fists. "If ye dinna take this wrapping from around my head, I'll do it myself. I canna bear this darkness any longer."

She grabbed his wrists and held them down by his sides, using her weight against his strength. "Ye will no'!" She knew he could break her grip with little effort, but she had to prevent him. "The healer said yer eyes must remain covered—both of them—if ye wish to regain yer sight."

"What sight?" he snarled. "She is blinding me as surely as that shattered sword did."

"A steel splinter went deep into yer left eye. She told ye, what one eye does, they both do, so to let yer wound heal, ye canna try to use the other." Ella released his wrists and placed a hand on his arm, still heavily muscled despite his forced inactivity. "Ye were out of yer head with fever for days—"

"What? The healer said 'twas mild."

"She sought to reassure ye. And the fever is done. So ye think all else is healed as well. But 'tis too soon. Do ye truly wish to lose yer eye?"

Calum was silent for a long moment before his shoulders dropped. "Nay," he bit out, defeated. "A blind scout is worthless, and a half blind man fares little better. If I am to be useful as a warrior..."

"Ye have been so patient," she said, cutting him off, and wishing she could do as he asked and reveal his gaze. She missed the way he looked at her. She heard the fear in his voice he struggled to hide. How he must long for the sight of blue skies...and everything else. "Ye can tolerate waiting a wee more."

He pressed his full lips together, then spoke. "If at the end, the reward is being able to see y..."

The abrupt end to his sentence made Ella study his face—as much as she could see for the bandages, her heart in her throat. Did he know her? After a moment, she rejected the thought. If he did, why would he continue to play along with her ruse? Still, once the healer removed the coverings from his eyes, how would seeing her again as Ella affect him? How angry would he be to know she was Janet? The tension in his jaw told her she'd only added to his misery today. "I am sorry. I did no' mean to make ye feel worse."

"I ken it, lass," he finally said. "'Tis no' yer fault the Lowlanders fight with poorly forged blades."

She encouraged him to move with a light tug on his arm. "Ye were unlucky to be so near to one that shattered," she said as they walked along. "But," she added as his fists clenched yet again, "ye were lucky to have made it home from the battle so quickly, and to be under the care of the Brodie healer. She saved yer life. She may well have saved yer sight. I hope so."

"No' half so much as I."

She squeezed his hand in sympathy. "We need to go in soon." She hesitated, then deliberately brightened her tone. "The Marymas feast is taking place this eve. Everyone is expected to attend. Ye, too." How she wanted him to be able to enjoy the celebration, to spend time with his friends, to laugh. She tensed, waiting for his response.

"Marymas? Already? How long have I been confined to that chamber?"

Ella sighed and walked on. He kept pace with her easily, despite the uneven ground. "Only a fortnight and a few days, Calum."

"So I'm to attend a feast I canna see and make a fool of myself trying to eat it?"

"I will be there to help ye."

He stopped again, head tilted back, face to the sky.

Whether in frustration or despair, behind the bandages, his eyes were probably squeezed shut. She could only imagine what kind of battle must be raging inside this proud man. She tried, but no amount of tugging would move him from this spot.

"Calum!" As Janet, she felt free to say his name more sharply than Ella ever would. "I've much to do before this eve. Will ye take me inside, please?" If his sense of humor failed, his sense of duty rarely did.

He took a breath and turned toward her. "Aye."

Relieved that he was moving, Ella guided him toward the keep's main door. Then her foot slipped on a patch of mud. She cried out, but before she fell to the ground, Calum scooped her up. He held her close against his chest, his arms solid supports across her back and behind her knees. Sudden heat coursed through her, whether from Calum's body or her own embarrassment, she couldn't say.

"Are ye hurt...Janet?"

Heart pounding, she shook her head, then remembered to speak. "Thanks to ye, Calum, nay. Ye saved me from falling. How did ye ken where I was?"

"I always ken where ye are." He started walking forward, still carrying her.

Ella shivered at the deep undertone of his voice rumbling through his chest and into her ribs, intensifying as it slipped deeper into her body. His words seemed to carry a promise she hoped for but dared not name.

But nay! Thanks to her altered voice and scent, he thought she was Janet, not Ella. How true was his love for her if he could speak so of Janet? She thought he loved her and her alone, yet it seemed he was no better than any of the men in her life. Faithless. Determined to have their way with any woman in reach. "Ye can put me down," she told him, guilt and anger stealing her enjoyment of his nearness. She must look ridiculous, being rescued by a blind man, no matter how good it felt to be held secure in his arms. No one else would know that angst filled her, but anyone could see them. Even now, the quiet bailey was too public a place for such a display.

"Are ye certain ye can remain standing?"

His tone was teasing, but his touch betrayed his concern, his hand on her back stroking up and down. He meant to soothe her, she knew, but his touch set her blood to singing. Yet he was flirting with Janet, not her. She fought down the feeling and took a breath. "Long enough to get inside, aye." Where she would find more onions.

He stood her on her feet and took her arm without further comment, but with a frown that made her fear that he'd been affected by holding her, too. Needing a distraction, she hurried them up the steps to the keep's heavy door and let him pull it open. Once he closed it behind them, his shoulders slumped and she realized he dreaded being confined indoors yet again.

She led him to the entrance to the great hall and paused. There was no one nearby. No one to call her by her name. She could remain Janet, at least for now. She didn't know what she would do if someone did forget their ruse and call her Ella. Admit to it, she supposed, and deal with Calum's reaction as she must.

"Take a breath," she told him. So soon after being in his arms, it might be a risk to emphasize his sense of smell, but she was confident the festival preparations would cover her scent. "Tell me what ye sense." His broad chest rose and fell, and watching him made her hungry to be held against it again. Even if only as Janet.

"People and hounds," he said, his fierce expression smoothing into enjoyment. "And for the Marymas, bannocks. Lots of them."

"And more?"

"The hearth fire burning, and..." He lifted his head, nostrils flaring while he took another breath.

He looked proud, strong and confident, despite the healer's bandages covering his eyes and wrapping around his dark head. "Roasting meats, aye, and tarts from the kitchen," he announced.

"I canna smell the pies, but all the rest, aye."

"Ye said my senses are undimmed. And I told ye, I notice everything." He turned his face to her. "I ken that Ella has been in my chamber, no' ye."

Ella froze. Nay, she'd been careful to keep the healer's herbs on her any time she tended him. Then she realized he did think of Ella and Janet as two different women and warm relief flooded her, easing the ache in her chest.

"I ken her scent. I told the healer I didna want her there."

"Perhaps ye only imagined...or something of her scent remains in the chamber from before the healer called me to ye."

Without the bandages over his eyes, she expected his

gaze would be locked with hers and her worries returned. Was he trying to tell her he knew—or at least suspected—who she really was? Could he truly find her scent among all the others in the keep?

"Perhaps."

Yet, as he held her safe in his arms, he'd hesitated before calling her Janet. Was he playing with her? That, she would not allow. She'd been through too much to be any man's plaything ever again.

"If she has been in yer chamber, 'twas not when I was present. And surely, she only means to help ye." She summoned a chuckle. "What man would object to another beautiful lass caring for him?"

Calum's mouth thinned and his fists clenched. "What good is beauty to a blind man? Can ye tell me that?"

His words hit her like a dirk to the heart. Was that all she meant to him? He saw only her beauty, but not who she was inside?

Nay, she would not accept that. His fear and frustration had set those resentful words spewing from his mouth. He'd pursued her from the moment he'd met her. He cared for her. He'd made his feelings for her plain. She had held him off, certain that she was not ready to be close to any man, even one who interested her, and who pursued her as consistently as Calum did.

Perhaps it was time to end this pretense. This false face she wore around him. She wanted to tell him the truth, but the great hall was no place for this conversation. This confrontation, if that was what it would become. She could not let him fall in love with Janet. It would hurt her too much. She knew that was selfish. She'd denied his advances again and again, but she did love him. She couldn't bear to lose him. He might be angry at her deception, but the Calum she knew would soon get past it.

Or would he? After succumbing to such a terrible injury, was he still the Calum she knew?

Who would Calum become if, as he feared, he'd lost half his sight? If he could not be the warrior he was before Harlaw, would he still be the man she loved? Friends had warned her he might be changed. Different. But she believed, deep inside, he would be the same man he'd always been, and he would adjust. Iain would see that he had an important place in the clan, no matter what. She would help.

So she must wait until the healer determined it was time to reveal his eye—and his future. The Marymas feast was a time to celebrate the Assumption, the coming harvest, and to prepare for the long winter ahead. It was also a celebration of good fortune. Of miracles. Ella hoped for two—that the love Calum once held in his heart for her remained, and that once his eyes were no longer covered, he would see on her face, in her eyes, the love she had hidden from him for too long.

———

CALUM DIDN'T KNOW HOW MUCH LONGER HE COULD STAND this. The enforced blindness was bad enough, but worse were these feelings for a woman who was not Ella.

Or was she? There were times he was convinced Ella attended him. At times, the onions Janet favored failed to completely mask her natural scent, and though rougher than Ella's, her touch seemed otherwise the same, even if the voice was altered.

Altered. Deliberately?

He'd held this woman in his arms minutes ago, more closely than he'd ever been able to hold Ella. He'd nestled her body against his chest, her heat warming his hands. Surely, he could not be this attracted to any other woman but his Ella.

Was Janet a mummery cooked up between Ella and the healer to circumvent his wish that Ella not be involved in his care?

Or was he days too late in that concern? She had been at his bedside when he awoke. Had she cared for him until he objected? Had she cared for him as a mother cares for a sick child? He couldn't bear the idea of it.

He was a warrior. A scout. And Ella was the woman he loved. The one that he wanted for his wife. That he wanted to bed, damn it. How was he to arouse her to accept him as a man if she'd cared for him while he was unconscious and helpless to control his body?

And what harm had he just done by his angry words? *What good was beauty to a blind man*, indeed? Yes, Ella was beautiful, but he loved all of her, not only her appearance. Her beauty encompassed who she was, how she cared for others—even for him, perhaps—and how she had fought for and protected herself at Ross.

Yet he'd told the truth. His angry outburst exposed his pain if he didn't get his sight back. If he lost his eye, his place in the clan, he'd have to give her up, too. She deserved to be with someone whole. The thought tore at his guts. He wanted her, but only if he remained the man he once was—with both eyes. He had to keep his distance until he knew who he would be, the warrior or the half-blind man.

But then, why the deception of Janet? If Ella was indeed pretending to be Janet, he didn't know what he would do.

He was confused and he knew it. And tired from the walk outside, which angered him again. How could he fight for his clan if a walk around the bailey exhausted him?

"I will return to my chamber now," he announced, not even certain Janet remained with him. She'd been silent since his angry comment.

"I'll take ye." Her voice had taken on a gruff edge. Had he hurt her feelings, then? Another reason to think this was Ella, not some fictional Janet.

"Nay, ye needna. Stay and enjoy the feast. I can find my way."

"Third door—"

"On the right. I ken it." He moved away without another word. He was at a loss for how to deal with Janet... or Ella...at this time. The healer had to take these bandages from his eyes. The deception they practiced would be impossible. And he would know whether he had two good eyes and the future he had worked for his entire life, or would be forgotten among the clan's crippled and ill, struggling to make use of any skills he retained.

It was a grim thought, and soured his mood further. He needed to *see*!

Where was the healer?

He stood still for a moment, orienting himself to the sounds and movement around him. Had he gotten turned around? Which way should he go? Ah, the great hall's hearth was ahead of him...there. The scent of burning wood was stronger in that direction. The way sound bounced around the hall, seeming farther away in that direction, told him the shape of the room. Which meant the herbal was to the left. He turned in that direction, going slowly so as to avoid barking his shins on a bench or tripping over a trestle table. People saw him coming, of course, and helped him avoid obstacles. He thanked them and moved on, embarrassed to be treated as one who could not take care of himself, even though he knew they meant their assistance as a kindness.

Could he face them with a warrior's pride once he could see again? Or worse, could he live among those who'd known him as a warrior when his sight was gone forever? That would be harder to survive than any battle he'd fought up to now. He must be freed from this darkness before he went mad.

The last helpful voice told him he'd reached the hallway he wanted. Once he'd successfully transited the great hall, getting to his objective was easy.

"Healer, are ye within?" He knew he'd come to the right place. The scents of herbs and flowers added to the often acrid or odorous potions and poultices she was constantly making, assaulted his nose.

"Good day to ye," he heard her say. "Where is Janet?"

He didn't let her use of the name distract him. "I left her to find her friends enjoying the feast, and came to find ye."

"Come in, then. There's a stool six paces ahead of ye to yer right hand. Have a seat and tell me what ye want."

"I want ye to remove these wrappings from my eyes," he said as he found the stool and settled one cheek on it, then slid over to sit on it fully. "It has been long enough."

"I'll be the judge of that."

He felt as much as heard the healer approach him. He fought to keep his voice calm and level as he told her, "If ye dinna remove them, I will. I've lived in darkness too long. I must ken what my future will be."

She stayed silent long enough that he began to sweat. Would she deny him?

"I will uncover yer eyes long enough to check the

injured one," she said. "But ye must accept that if I dinna like what I see, I may have to cover it yet again."

"Please. Dinna do that." He couldn't believe he'd been reduced to begging, but that was what blind men did, was it not? Only he would not be blind, merely one-eyed, if the healing had not gone well.

"Turn yer head this way. Ye will keep yer eyes closed," she ordered as she clipped the binding around his head and unwound it.

The feel of cool air on the skin of his face that, except for brief periods when she changed the bandages, she'd kept covered for weeks nearly undid him.

"Eyes closed," she reminded him, then removed the pad over his damaged eye. "I'm going to touch yer eyelid," she warned, slid a warm finger down from his eyebrow and pulled up the lid.

Brightness assaulted him, but he reveled in it.

"Hmmm. What do ye see?"

"Light. Brightness. How is it?"

She let go of his lid. "Keep it closed."

He was happy to comply, wincing against the sting of tears the sudden brightness had elicited. But her failure to answer him made his gut tense.

She removed the pad from his other eye. "Verra well. Open them slowly," she ordered.

At first, the light was too much, though she'd taken care to face him toward a dark corner of the herbal and not looking toward the hearth or any candle flames.

His eyes teared, but he blinked and cleared them. Slowly, things came into focus. Both eyes or just the good one? He closed that lid and found he could still make out objects in front of him. Relief filled him, so profound that it made his chest heavy, his arms leaden weights he couldn't lift.

"I can see with the injured one." He turned to her voice. "I see ye. A little blurry—"

"That is to be expected. Do ye still have pain?"

"Only a little."

"Good. I am not surprised the light seems strong now. Ye will adjust to it as yer vision clears."

"That is good to hear," he said, his words heartfelt. But he had to know something else, too. "Now, tell me the truth before I have to see for myself," he demanded, but lowered his voice when her eyes widened. He was not here to frighten her, but he needed answers. "Ella and Janet are the same person." He didn't make it a question.

The healer pinked and glanced aside. "Ye suspected so."

"I did, though not right away."

Her reluctance to answer told him everything he needed to know. She had lied to him. So had Ella. But the anger twisting his gut told him no matter how much he condemned what they had done, he had allowed himself to be deceived. He'd known all along that Janet was Ella, so he could only be angry in some small portion with them.

Most of his ire he directed at himself. And he didn't know what to do about any of it.

––––––––––

ELLA SAT AT A TABLE WITH SOME OF HER FRIENDS, BUT instead of talking and laughing with them, she could not take her gaze away from Calum making his careful way across the great hall. She feared he would meet with disaster—a fall or some other embarrassment—but pride in him filled her that he would attempt it. Others helped him avoid hazards with a word or two. Those he accepted with more grace than she thought he would be able to summon. His determination and adaptability continued to impress her. But knowing where he was headed—to beard the healer in her own den—scared her.

She prayed his eye had healed well enough to let him understand that the future he'd expected to have was not lost. That he would still be a warrior for the clan. A man in the way he understood manhood.

If he lost the eye, could he adapt to that? She hoped he never had to find out.

She also prayed the healer did not admit the Janet ruse. If she did, what would Calum do about it? Accept that she'd do anything to take care of him, including lie to him? Or reject her for her subterfuge?

She couldn't sit here waiting for the axe to fall. Without a word, she left her friends and followed Calum's path across the hall, then waited silently by the door while the healer removed his coverings, and rejoiced at the vision he described. *He could see.*

She needed to wash the onion scent from her hands and breath before he saw her. And perhaps some cream would soften the damage the lye had done to her hands. She started to back away from the door but her boot scraped on the flagstones.

Calum turned at the sound, this time with his eyes open. "Ella. I see ye."

She was out of time. She went to him, hands out to grasp his if he raised them, or to give him a hug full of joy and relief. "I'm so glad ye do," she said when he let her capture his fingers. Then the tone he had used sank in. "Is aught amiss?"

He lifted her hands and sniffed, then pulled his fingers free. "Will ye remain Ella now?" When his brow lowered and he glanced aside at the healer, she realized he knew about their deception before she arrived.

Ella's belly plunged as if into a frigid lake. She glanced at the older woman, who shook her head.

She had no choice. If she dreamed of having any future with this man, she must admit what she'd done, and hope he understood why she'd done it.

"Calum, I couldna bear to see ye suffering," she began. "I helped care for ye before ye woke up. We...I...created Janet so that ye would allow me to remain at yer side, where I needed to be. Where I thought I belonged."

"Did ye think so? Ye lied to me."

How could his newly revealed visage be so full of censure? How dare he condemn her for caring for him? If this was going to be their future—if she made such an effort and he reacted like he'd rather die than accept her help—maybe she'd been wrong about him.

"I did everything to help ye heal. And to help ye see again. If ye canna forgive that—"

"Ye believed I would thank ye for seeing me as helpless as a bairn?" The flat tone had a definite chill to it.

Ella crossed her arms and wrapped her hands around them for warmth and protection. "Like ye are behaving now?" She shook her head as he stood. To make her look up at him? "I never meant to do that. I love ye."

"If ye truly did, ye wouldna have tried to fool me. Playing such games with a man in my condition is a kind of torture. Losing my sight wasna enough for ye? Ye had to make me fear I was losing my mind with yer deception?"

"Calum," the healer interjected, "Ella helped me care for ye. There is nay shame in that. She lied to protect ye, and that is the only reason. She proved her loyalty to ye. Dinna blame her, for I went along with the ruse. I helped her craft it. Blame me for not having a better answer to the question of how to keep ye safe."

Calum studied the older woman for a long moment. "And after that, I am supposed to trust either of ye?" He huffed out a breath. "Am I free to go?"

"I must cover the injured eye again so ye dinna damage it while ye sleep."

"Nay."

"I willna cover both. 'Tis time for ye to start using yer eyes again. Ye can uncover it in the morning. We'll do that for the next sennight. After that, it should be healed well enough that ye may sleep without protecting it. And yer vision should continue to improve."

He sat back on the stool without another objection and let her tend him while Ella watched. She felt frozen to the floor, unable to move, either to go to him or to leave. When the healer finished, he stood and walked out of the herbal without another glance or word to either of them.

Ella sank onto the stool Calum had vacated. "He willna forgive me." She kept her tone matter-of-fact, but inside, her heart was in pieces. Sharp, jagged little pieces that cut with every breath she took. "Am I never to find a man who accepts me—all of me—for who I am?"

The healer pressed her lips together and raised a finger. "Dinna let him belittle ye. Without ye, he wouldna have regained his sight."

"I dinna think he will believe that. Ye are the healer."

"Perhaps as his eyesight clears and he regains his confidence, he will accept the part ye played in his recovery. He is still hurt and embarrassed by it all, but that will pass."

"Will it? Will he come to me and beg my forgiveness? After this, I canna...I willna go to him."

The healer pressed her lips together and nodded, then

captured Ella's gaze with her own. "If he doesna, there is yer answer. Ye have been strong for him, but ye must be stronger still for yerself. He will come to ye, or ye will tire of waiting and find what ye seek in another man."

"I dinna want another," Ella said, turning to stare out the doorway Calum had exited, the pieces of her heart a leaden weight in the bottom of her chest. "I thought I'd found what I needed in Calum. I hope that I still can. That he will come to see I did the best I could for him. I will fight for him—for us. But if I must," she vowed, "I will find my way forward without him."

HIGHLAND YULETIDE REUNION

Cameron Sutherland and Mary Elizabeth Rose meet in HIS HIGHLAND LOVE (His Highland Heart Series, Book 3) when he comes to Clan Rose after being injured protecting Catherine Rose and Kenneth Brodie. Cam and Mary's romance comes to fruition as she cares for him in HIS HIGHLAND BRIDE (His Highland Heart Series Book 4).

In this story, Mary's sisters and their families return to Rose for Cameron and Mary's first Yuletide as a married couple—and the first for Mary as Laird of Rose. With so much family underfoot and preparations underway for the celebration, will they have any time together? I hope this glimpse puts you in the mood to celebrate the Yuletide season with the special people in your life.

SCOTTISH HIGHLANDS, YULETIDE, 1412

"They're coming!" Mary Rose burst into the Clan Rose library waving a parchment, blue eyes wide and bright.

Cameron Sutherland set his book aside and glanced out the window at the waning wintry light, expecting to see riders approaching the gate. He saw nothing but snow streaked with pink by the setting sun and the deep green fir and pine forest beyond, so he rose and stepped toward his excited bride. "Who is coming, Mary my love? And when?" He reached out to brush a blonde curl from her shoulder just as Mary thrust the parchment toward him.

"My sisters are coming. With their families. A Brodie rider just delivered Annie's letter." Mary clasped her hands over her heart. "Ach, Cam, I'm so excited to see them and wee Ewan. I canna wait for the next fortnight to pass."

Cam glanced at the bottom of the page while Mary

talked. Signed by Annie, Lady Brodie, with the Brodie seal stamped in the wax. "I thought I heard someone ride in. This explains why the guard didn't send for me." He gestured with the parchment. "The rider brought this news for ye."

"For both of us, husband."

He set the letter on top of his book, certain that Mary would rather tell him the rest than have him read the details. "Does she say why they dinna plan to come sooner? We are only a day's hard ride away."

"They're having an early Yule celebration at Brodie first. Since Annie and Iain are bringing their wee son, they canna make the trip in one day. Kenneth and Cat will travel with them, along with an escort."

"Aye, of course." Though Rose and Brodie shared a border, travel in the Highlands was never safe, especially with the approach of midwinter.

"Ach, what if it snows again? They'll be delayed even more."

"Dinna fash, wife. They'll get here, no matter the weather. And they'll make our first Yule even more joyful than we planned." Cam knew his bride. Preparing for her sisters' visit would keep her floating on clouds for the next fortnight. Her mind was surely spinning with ideas and chores enough to keep the entire clan busy until their guests—nay, their family—arrived. He took her hand in his larger ones. "What do we need to do first?"

Mary's lips formed an "O" and she gestured toward the

parchment. "I must set down every idea," she said, her gaze drifting aside in thought. "What needs to be done, and when, in the keep and without. Cleaning. Making sure things are put out of wee Ewan's reach so he doesn't get into mischief. Decorating the hall for Yule."

Cam nodded, caught up in the spirit of Mary's musing. "If Rose does as Sutherland does every year, we'll need boughs of fir, sprigs of holly..."

"Aye, of course. Those will make the great hall smell heavenly!"

"But gathering them could wait until everyone arrives. Yer sisters might enjoy finishing the decorations in their childhood home. Iain and Kenneth can help me bring in a suitable Yule log for the great hall's hearth. And we'll need to plan hunts to keep them entertained."

"And everyone fed, aye. I must speak with Cook right away. Ach, we've so many things to do!"

Cameron pulled his wife into his arms while a vision of apple cakes sweetened with honey danced in his head. They'd been a favorite of his growing up, but did the Rose cook know how to make them? He'd ask her later. Right now, Mary was in his arms, needing him. "Wheesht, Mary my love. Ye dinna have to arrange it all right this minute."

"Nay, but ye ken how my mind works."

"That I do. And I ken ye will put all in perfect order. The entire clan will help. We will do what ye wish, when ye wish it." With one finger, he lifted her chin, then gazed deep into her eyes. "But there's something I want ye to include as ye note each need," he said, pulling himself from the blue depths he loved.

"There is?" Her brow furrowed and she stiffened in his arms.

"Aye." Cam fought to hide a grin. He never intruded on Mary's running of the keep, so he knew this demand surprised her. He hoped she'd like his request. "I wish for ye to put time for us in yer plans, wife. I willna have ye disappear from me for the next fortnight while ye set all to rights."

She softened in his arms, a smile lighting her face as she nodded. "I could never disappear from ye, my laird. Nor ye from me. We will have our time, never fear."

"'Tis a promise, and I want a kiss to seal it." He tightened his hold on her, then lifted her and swung her around.

She shrieked with laughter, then gasped, "Cam, put me down! Ye are making me dizzy."

He set her on her feet but kept her secure in his embrace. "I willna release ye until ye kiss me," he threatened.

She placed two fingers over his lips before he could swoop in and claim her mouth. "But we have nay mistletoe," she teased.

"'Tis no' the Yuletide, yet, Mary my love. We dinna need it now. But ye will gather mistletoe. Lots of mistletoe. And hang it throughout the keep. I intend to kiss ye soundly wherever I find ye."

"And I, to kiss ye back." She proceeded to do just that.

When Cam finally came up for air, he had more than kissing on his mind. "Do we have time for us now, my lady wife?"

"Hmmm." She tilted her head and tapped her temple. "I dinna believe that is on any tally I've yet begun, my laird. But with the right encouragement, I could be convinced to add it."

"Then let me encourage ye," Cam said and took her lips again. When Mary melted even deeper into his embrace, he scooped her up, then set her on the library table.

"Cam! Nay, no' here. The servants..."

"Will no' come near, but I will lock the door for milady's peace of mind." He left her long enough to make certain they would not be disturbed, then returned to his wife.

Mary reached for him, her expression full of love and longing. "How will we find moments like this with half of clan Brodie underfoot?"

"'Tis our home, Mary. We ken all the best places to hide..."

"Ye forget," Mary said, her voice bright with mirth, "my sisters do as well." She hugged him tightly as she chuckled, then sobered and captured his gaze. "We are about to celebrate our first Yule as man and wife. My sisters and their families will make it even more special, but while they are with us, I need ye to recall how grateful I am for ye." She laid a hand on his cheek. "Ye will be at the top of every note I write, my first thought every morn and my last thought each night. I love ye, Cameron Sutherland."

Cam couldn't hold back the answering swell of love and contentment that filled his heart, nor did he want to. "And I love ye, Mary Elizabeth Rose. Ye are the best part of me." His life, once nearly lost, had begun again with this woman. He needed her more than he knew how to tell her, but he had to try. "I ken 'tis early to say this, but I wish this to be the happiest Yule of yer life, the first of many we share together."

"I do, too, Cam. Each more filled with love and laughter as the years go by," Mary replied. "Happy Yule, my love."

———

"There's a likely looking tree," Cameron Sutherland said the next day to his best friend at Rose, one of his guard captains, Paton.

"Aye," the man agreed. Two years younger than Cameron, Paton was a recent addition to the clan, though he'd fostered at Sutherland. He'd come from the islands with Domnhall's army and decided to stay. His skill with weapons and ability to lead men made him rise quickly through the Rose ranks and put him in Cameron's company often enough to renew the childhood bond between the two men. "'Twill take a dozen men to move it once we cut the bloody thing down. Is there nay a tree closer to the keep that will do as well?"

Cameron scratched his head. "I dinna ken," he said in a rising tone of amazement. "Why didna I think to look there first?"

Paton punched his shoulder and laughed. "Verra well. This one will do. Anything to make the laird happy during her family's visit."

"I fear it will take more than the perfect Yule log," Cameron said, then immediately wished he'd kept his mouth shut. Paton had the gift of reading people, one of the reasons he was a good leader.

"Trouble *dans la famille*?"

Cameron winced and shrugged. He might as well say it. Paton might have some ideas for how to ease any pain Mary would feel. "I love Mary Elizabeth Rose with every fiber of my being. And to a lesser extent, her sisters and their families, as well. But the impending visit *fashes* me."

"Why? From all I've heard, the sisters were united—"

"Against their father, aye. But now, her sisters are wed and Annie has a son. Things have changed."

"Is that all?"

"Well, of course 'tis nay all."

"So ye're *fashed* because ye two have yet to be blessed with an heir to Rose. Is that it?"

"In the month since we wed? Are ye daft? I fear that despite her excitement over the visit, she'll be disappointed. The changes in her family will overwhelm her.

Rose is their home nay longer and that will make a difference to all of them. Thanks to her da, Mary had years of practice hiding her dismay from everyone." Everyone but him, he meant. He knew her too well to let her suffer when she intended to enjoy the coming invasion of her family. She was excited and had the entire keep humming with preparations for the big event. For her, that big event was their arrival more than the Yule celebration. "I dinna ken what to do for her," he finally admitted.

"Have ye talked to her about this?"

"Nay. I dinna want to plant the idea and have it grow. If she truly doesna mind, I dinna want her thinking that I do."

Paton nodded. "Then keep that thought in yer mind at all times. If ye let her see ye *fashing*, she'll want to ken why, to help ye, and that will lead—"

"Nowhere I want to go, aye." Cameron shrugged and began to walk around the tree. It was a fine specimen, big enough to burn for the twelve days of the Yule celebration. "We'll come back with more men tomorrow," he decided, "and take it down so it will have time to dry."

Paton took the hint and changed the subject, going on and on about a lass he'd lately had his eye on while they trudged back to the keep. Cameron let him talk but paid little attention. He felt better for having told Paton his fears, but he still didn't know what to do if the impending visit was not all that Mary hoped it would be.

———

THE BAILEY RANG WITH LAUGHTER AND SHOUTED GREETINGS as Mary's sisters arrived. She joined in the laughter as Cat dismounted and was immediately surrounded by old friends. Her sisters had come home to people they'd grown up with. People who were happy to see them. Mary couldn't contain her joy and embraced first Annie, then, once Cat made her way out of the crush, her youngest sister. Iain approached next, eight-month-old Ewan squirming in his arms. "He wants down," Iain announced, as if it was not obvious to all.

"He willna stop until he's on the floor," Annie said, taking the wean from her husband. "Then ye crawl so fast, I have to chase ye," she added, chucking her son under his chin until he rewarded her with a grin. "He's so active, as soon as he finishes one meal, he's asking for the next. Iain says he was like that, too, so I expect Ewan will grow out of it, but we'd best warn Cook we could pester her from morning till night."

"I'm sure Cook can handle him," Mary assured her, then turned to Cat. "Was the trip difficult for ye?"

"Nay, everyone is fine." Cat turned and smiled at her husband as Kenneth came up and put an arm around her waist.

"Everyone needs to rest a wee before the celebrations start," Kenneth said with a glance at Cat's belly.

"Are ye—" Mary started, and then stopped. Despite her

eagerness to know if Kenneth meant her youngest sister was with child, she should let them announce it in their own way. "*Dinna fash*," Mary said instead. "Let's go inside and get everyone settled. We'll have plenty of time to catch up."

"Where is Cameron?" Kenneth looked around, then spotted him. "Ah, helping with the horses, of course. Iain, let's go give him a hand with the wagons."

With that, the two men made their escape, leaving Mary's sisters and wee Ewan to go inside with her.

Mary chose to keep that evening's dinner simple and light. The travelers were tired and would need to find their beds. Ewan was safely ensconced in the nursery with the clan's other bairns so that the parents could have a restful night. When the meal ended, the men gathered by the hearth fire with their ales. Mary took her sisters up to her old room, the one Annie and Iain would share. She and Cameron now used the laird's chamber. Annie headed straight for the window seat while she and Cat settled side by side on the edge of the bed.

Save for the Brodie traveling cases stacked against one wall, the chamber was the same as if the last few months had never happened. She and her sisters sat in their usual places in the room Mary had grown up in, where they always went to share problems, heartbreaks, and happiness. Mary hoped the latter was on tonight's agenda. She waited, not sure who would start.

Annie, of course.

"So, how is married life?" Her middle sister asked with a smile.

"Wonderful," Mary said. "Exciting. Exhausting. Or maybe that has more to do with being laird."

"Likely," Cat interjected. "Though ye have done the job for Da for several years. And now ye have Cameron to help ye. So what about yer life now is exhausting ye?"

Her smirk told Mary what she was thinking. She and Cam were still newlyweds, after all.

"Leave Mary alone," Annie warned. "Ye and Kenneth are much the same."

"It was so romantic. A double wedding! I never dreamed mine could be shared with my sisters in that way," Cat rhapsodized. "I'm glad we live as close together as we do. If Da had his way, we'd be scattered across Scotland."

"Or gone nowhere at all," Annie reminded her with a nod to Mary. "It has been a momentous year."

"And now with Yuletide upon us, we can be together again," Cat said, then yawned. "But I think rest is first on the list."

Cat wasn't going to share her news with them? Mary hid her disappointment, still determined to let Cat tell them in her own way. "For ye two, aye," Mary said. "I've a keep to run and hungry family to feed on the morrow." She yawned and stood. "I will bid ye good night. I'm so glad ye are here. I hope ye ken that."

Cat and Annie stood, too. "Of course we do. We will get

busy with the preparations tomorrow," Annie told her, then she, too, yawned. "I guess that makes it unanimous. Get some sleep." With that she winked and Cat burst out laughing.

Mary laughed, too, all the way to the laird's chamber she now shared with Cameron. "Ye are here! I thought ye would still be drinking and telling tales with Iain and Kenneth."

"They hid it well, but they were worn out from the journey. Riding alone, they would have been here much faster, but wagons for the things the lasses and a bairn need made for a longer trek. They went to check on their horses, but they'll be in their chambers soon." He took Mary in his arms. "And ye ken what that means, Mary my love. Ye have reached the end of yer list for the day. All except for the most important thing."

"Truly? Whatever could that be?"

Cameron dipped his head and brushed her lips with his. "Does this remind ye?"

The scent of ale filled her nose. "Ach, aye. We need more mint."

"How about this?" He trailed his tongue down the side of Mary's throat and gently bit where it joined her shoulder.

"Ye lads need to hunt tomorrow?"

"And this?" He lifted her skirt and traced his hand up the outside of her leg to her hip.

"Hmmm...'tis beginning to come to me."

"I'll see that it does," Cam promised.

Someone knocked on the door.

"Whoever that is, I'm going to kill them," Cam said, dropping Mary's skirt and releasing her. He went to the door and flung it open.

"I'm so sorry to bother ye," Annie said, "but Iain just returned from the stable and sent me to tell ye one of yer mares has a swollen knee."

"Why did he send ye and nay come himself?"

Annie grinned. "He feared he might ah...interrupt ye..."

Cam bit his lip on what he wanted to say about Iain's equine observational skills—and his timing.

"The mare twisted her knee yesterday. The stable master is aware and caring for her." The Rose stable master also had plenty of well-trained lads to help him and didn't need Cameron—or Iain Brodie—second-guessing his decisions. "But thank Iain for us, Annie. Good night."

"Ye are nay going—"

Cam glanced around at Mary, who stood by the bed watching him deal with her sister and laughing at him. Nay, not out loud, but amusement shone from her eyes.

"I'll check with the stable master in the morning. Thank ye, Annie. Good night." Cam closed the door.

Annie immediately knocked and forced him to open it again. "Aye?"

"Good night to ye both, too." She gave Mary a bright grin and went on her way down the hall.

Cam closed the door and put the bar across it. "Nay more interruptions, Mary my love."

She went into his arms. "They've had their fun, so I think no'."

———

THE NEXT DAY, WHILE THE MEN WERE OUT OF THE KEEP stripping the branches and bark from the tree Cam and Paton had chosen, preparing it for the hearth, Mary and some of the lasses ventured out to collect evergreen boughs for the great hall. By the time they finished, evening approached and Mary checked with Cook to ensure supper would be ready when the men returned. Before long, the keep's heavy door swung open. A dozen men waited there, Paton, Iain and Kenneth included, carrying the huge log between them on their shoulders, Cam at the fore.

"Clear the way for the Yule log," Cameron called out. "'Tis here to bring good luck into the keep for the new year!"

Mary smiled. Cameron had such a way of making everything better. Her da had simply seen it carried in and placed into the hearth. Cam's announcement made it more of an event.

Everyone shifted to the walls, pushing aside any

remaining benches between the door and the hearth. Tables had already been pushed back, and people lined the path toward the hearth, smiling in anticipation.

In contrast, the men carried the log between them with solemn ceremony. Once they laid the biggest end of it in place on glowing coals, Kenneth turned and gave Cat a wink, and Iain smiled at Annie. Cameron beckoned to the healer, who anointed the log with a concoction made of wine and herbs that would scent the hall and help the log catch fire. The rest of the log extended out onto the hearthstone and beyond that onto the great hall's stone floor where rushes had been swept well clear. Each day, the log would be pushed farther into the fire as it burned away.

Before the evening meal, once the tables and benches had been moved back into place, and to the cheers of the assembled clan and guests, some of the clan's older children adorned the log with pinecones, holly berries, and slices of dried apples, gifts to any deities that might grant the clan good luck. Then, to help the log catch fire, men piled kindling on the coals on either side of it.

When all was ready, Mary's heart beat faster as she contemplated the role she had assumed for the clan. It was the laird's responsibility to light the Yule log, and by doing so, to bring good fortune for the coming year. Somehow, this simple celebration, made with solemnity, but also with great joy and hope, brought her role home to her in a way that gave her chills as nothing else had done since her father's passing. She took a breath, glanced at Cameron for strength, and received it from his encouraging smile, then lit a torch made from the remains of last year's Yule log in the coals of the hearth fire. She touched it to the head of this year's log where the healer's wine mixture flared up, then lit the kindling, and finally, laid the torch on the now-burning Yule log. "May by this act the gods of Yule bring joy, peace, and prosperity to our clans now and for the next year, till we celebrate again," she said, and felt a sense of peace and satisfaction fill her.

"'Tis perfect!" Cat exclaimed.

Cameron moved behind Mary, wrapped his arms around her, and for a moment, rested his chin on her head. "Well done, lass," he whispered into her hair.

"Ye, too, my love," she told him, nodding at the cheerful blaze in the hearth. "Ye chose well." Mary agreed with her youngest sister's sentiment. Cam had chosen a grand log that would carry them through the twelve days of Yuletide, with some left for next year's torch.

Cameron turned her to look at him. "I did, indeed, Mary my love, when I chose ye." In front of the entire clan, he bent his head and kissed her.

Lost in the joy of the moment, Mary kissed him back.

Later, while they ate supper, she confided, "I hope last year's luck doesna carry over from its torch."

"Nay? Other than me nearly dying, and ye losing yer da, oh, and the Grant conspiracy to take over Rose, I thought 'twas a great year." At Mary's disbelieving frown, he added, "After all, I won ye, and we are wed, Mary my love. 'Twas a year I will remember with joy till my dying day."

"Ye make a good point," Mary conceded with a smile and a kiss for his reminder to look on the bright side. "I hope ye have a very long memory."

After supper, while Cameron dealt with a summons from the stable master, Mary met with Cook, then headed to their chamber. Her husband hadn't returned yet, so she readied herself for bed, already thinking ahead to what she planned for the next day. She fell asleep mid-list and woke to the sun shining through gaps around the edges of the window covers.

Cameron still lay beside her.

"'Tis early yet, Mary my love," he told her, taking her hand in his. "Ye needna get up right away."

"What about ye?" She turned to him and ran a finger down his cheek, then cupped his chin.

Cam reached for her, and she went into his arms without another thought for what the day would bring. This man made her happier than she'd ever dreamed possible.

"I treasure every moment of our time together," Cam told her.

"As I treasure ye."

When Mary and Cam made their way downstairs, they heard that some of the women had headed out into the woods soon after sunup to collect mistletoe and holly. The lasses returned, laughing and chattering like birds with the first of their harvest as she and Cam finished breaking their fast, then headed out again. Other women brought out stores of ribbon and lace, and some came from their crofts bringing bread and cakes to add to what Cook could produce. A little later, the men went hunting while the women saw to decorating the great hall, laughing while they worked, some humming or singing. Mary and her sisters joined in, each taking on a different task to help the other lasses in the clan, but sharing pleased looks as they saw how much the clan seemed to be enjoying this time together.

"'Tis because of ye," Annie confided softly at one point when she and Mary stood to the side, looking over the decorations going up in the great hall. "The change in everyone since ye and Cam took over is clear to me, even if ye dinna see it yet."

Mary's heart lifted. She did see how much happier everyone seemed. "I'd like to accept that, but I canna take all the credit. Cam has much to do with the changes. Perhaps even more than I. They are used to me. He has made the difference. And they're happy to see ye and Cat, too, ye ken."

Annie hugged her and they went back to work.

———

ONCE HE RETURNED FROM THE HUNT, CAMERON CORNERED Mary outside the kitchen where an alcove hid them from view, wrapped her in his arms and kissed her, then did it again. "I missed ye," he admitted. "And I'm here to make certain ye have me on yer list for today. And some time to rest."

"Always, my love," she answered and captured his lips. "Thank ye for making this a wonderful Yuletide," she told him after they came up for air.

Clearly she misunderstood what he meant by rest, but he wouldn't push the point when she seemed so happy. "As ye have, too, Mary my love," he said, wondering what had brought such gratitude to the fore, but grateful his kisses were met with even more enthusiasm than usual. He could happily kiss Mary all the rest of the day and into the night. But at the moment, he'd rather take her upstairs. Without mentioning his concern for her, he could help her rest by making love to her and make certain she melted in his arms.

Until they heard Annie scream.

"Ewan, come back here! Close the door. Dinna let him get outside!"

Mary put her hands on either side of Cam's face. "Ye ken I must go..."

He sighed and stepped back, allowing her to slip by him and run to the great hall to help her sister.

The rest of the sennight went much the same. Just as he got a few minutes with Mary, someone would come to say they'd run out of ribbons for the extra garlands they were making, or Cook needed a few minutes of her time, or Kenneth wanted to challenge him to a test of skill of one sort or another, or Iain thought they needed to go hunting again. Keeping their guests, nay, their family, entertained became more and more a burden as the week went by. Not that he'd ever admit that to Mary. Paton had warned him again to keep his frustration to himself. Apparently he had not hidden it as well as he thought if his friend noticed. Mary, thankfully, was too distracted, and probably too tired, to do so. That concerned him, but he contented himself with watching out for her and making certain she rested once each day was done.

On the tenth day of Yule, Cam hadn't seen Mary since the morning before, but not because of their family. He and his men been called out to help fight a fire in a nearby croft. Putting out the fire, and then getting that family temporarily resettled with another crofter kept him away from the keep until after sunrise. By the time he got back, cleaned up, and fell into bed, Mary was up and gone, dealing with whatever she needed to deal with for the day. He slept for several hours, then woke, missing her.

Very well, he knew how to solve this problem. He marched down to the laird's solar, intending to corner Mary there, convince her to interrupt her work, and let her have her way with him.

When he got to the closed door, he heard voices and realized Mary wasn't alone. He recognized the other voice coming through the door. Cat was there, and the two were giggling like wee lasses playing with their dollies. Did he hear Annie, too? He rested his head against the thick oak barrier for as long as it took to take a deep breath and let it out. He hadn't had this much trouble getting Mary alone when her da was alive and determined to keep them apart. Time with her sisters was precious, but if he could find her damned lists, he'd cross a few other things off and write his name in the spaces he made. At least his early fears about Mary being disappointed with her sisters' visit had been unfounded. He took comfort in that and headed for the practice ground to work off his frustration.

———

THE LAST DAY OF YULETIDE ARRIVED WITH A LIGHT snowfall that freshened the frosting on the evergreen trees and gave the world outside a peaceful silence. Mary enjoyed it from the window in their chamber after she stirred their fire, then returned to bed where Cam waited for her.

He pulled her to him and wrapped her in his arms, warming her from the cold breeze that had blown snowflakes into her hair through the window. "All's quiet?"

"Aye, for now. Before long, wee Ewan will be up in the nursery and his parents will be in the great hall, breaking their fast. Which is where we should go—"

"No' yet, Mary my love. I'm nay finished warming ye."

She rolled within his arms and gave him a kiss. "Nay, ye havena. But I ken ye have much to do—"

"Naught that canna wait while I take care of the woman I love," he answered and shifted her more fully on top of him, pulled the covers up to her shoulders, then laughed when she sat up, straddling him, and they fell to his thighs. They took their time, loving each other as they had learned to do after months of waiting to be wed, slowly and with complete attention. When they finished, Mary stretched out on Cameron's chest and tucked her head between his shoulder and neck, content to enjoy their closeness. They hadn't been as successful at keeping each other at the top of the list as she'd promised when the news came about her sisters' visit. But they'd managed as well as could be expected. As long as Cam was happy, she was, too.

"Are ye pleased with how the visit has gone?" He asked, seeming to read her mind.

"Save for not entirely keeping my promise to ye, aye. I'll be sad to see them go tomorrow."

"Next year, we will visit them," Cam vowed. "'Twill be easier on everyone."

"On them, certainly. Ewan will be walking by then, and there may be more Brodie bairns in the family. Still, 'twill nay be so easy on us as ye think, husband."

"Nay? Why no'? If they must deal with all the other arrangements, we can keep busy, or we can rest, as we wish."

She sat up and put his hand on her belly. "We'll have plenty to keep us busy, never fear."

"A bairn?" Cam's eyes widened, and when she nodded, his bright smile nearly blinded her.

"Ach, Mary my love, a bairn. Our bairn."

Her heart swelled when she found tears glinting in his eyes.

"'Twill be an heir for Rose, and another cousin for Sutherland and for Brodie. Else I'd suggest making the trip to Sutherland to visit yer family next year, but it may prove more difficult with a wee bairn."

"How long have ye kenned?"

"Only two days. I waited so I could tell ye as a Yule gift."

"I heard ye and Cat laughing in yer solar two days ago. Ye told her?"

"Aye, Annie was there, too. I ken I should have told ye first, but—"

"Nay, ye did right, Mary my love. I dinna mind ye sharing the news with yer sisters. I do mind them keeping it from me. Ye'd think one of them—or their husbands—would let slip the news."

"Iain and Kenneth dinna ken. This was a secret between sisters until the time was right to tell ye. Cat has good news, as well."

He took her hand and kissed it. "I'm glad. When will ye tell the clan?"

"Tonight, at the celebration. The entire clan will be there, including those from the nearby crofts and some from farther away. 'Twill be their lairds' gift to them, as well. From both of us."

"I canna think of a better one," Cam told her and pulled her down onto his chest again.

Mary reveled in his warmth and the feel of his strength under her fingertips. Her husband. The man she loved more than anything in the world.

The rest of the day went smoothly. Mary's lists had ensured preparations were complete and well done. When all was ready, she opened the buttery and had the men bring out casks of ale and wine. Cook outdid herself with the dinner and the sweets that followed it. Only the prospect of her sisters and their families leaving on the morrow added a dispiriting flavor to Mary's enjoyment of the evening. But she soon forgot that as everyone pushed back the tables and cleared the floor for dancing. The Yule log fit neatly into the great hall's hearth by this evening, so no one was going to trip over it, no matter how crowded the dancing became.

She pulled her sisters to her for a hug before releasing them to their husbands and turning to Cameron. "Shall we dance?"

In answer, he took her hand a led her to the floor.

That night, what she had expected to be a celebration with her sisters and their families in the Rose keep became a clan celebration with the keep and crofters. With a glad heart, she vowed it would become the way Rose celebrated Yuletide for years to come.

HEART OF ICE

This story is set nearly a year before the prequel to my Highland Talents series, HEART OF STONE. In this story, at an important event in Clan MacNabb—the birth of the first child to eldest son and heir, Keenan, and his wife—we meet Fenella Leny MacNabb, who has an understanding of a future with Gavan, the laird's middle son. If you've read HEART OF STONE, you know Fenella and Gavan's relationship stumbles, but at this point, she awaits his return from his wanderings, and she struggles with both joy for and envy of the happy couple and the impending birth.

If you haven't read HEART OF STONE, I recommend you get it and read it after this story, but before the next one.

Fennella McNabb was visiting with her friend the weaver in the nearby village when a lad ran past, doubled back and cried into the doorway, "Keenan's wife is laboring. The heir's bairn is on the way! Pray for them!"

He waved at them and continue on, shouting the good news to alert the entire village. He'd be tired—and hoarse—if he meant to reach some of the outlying crofts, but Fenella doubted he needed to make the effort. In the area around the MacNabb keep, rumors were known to spread quickly. By evening, there would be few associated with the clan who lacked the news. Most would make their way to the great hall or in the clan's small kirk, heads bent in prayer for the safe delivery of this child.

Everyone would want to know about the heir's first bairn, be it a lad or a lass. While only a lad could become the next heir in MacNabb after his grandda and da, a lass who took after her beautiful mother and handsome da would make a strong alliance some day for MacNabb with her marriage.

"Well, 'tis about time. By my reckoning, the bairn is a few days late," the weaver told Fenella.

"Are ye taking over care of the clan from the healer, then?" Fenella teased her with a smile. "Or only the expectant mothers?" The weaver and the healer were the same age and friends of long-standing, but each kept to their own specialty and were masters—or mistresses—of their craft.

"'Tis what she told me," the weaver admitted with a shrug. "She's always a wee bit concerned, ye ken, when a bairn takes its time."

"Many bairns seem to come late—or early. The mother doesna always ken exactly when—"

"I ken that. As does the healer. But Keenan was away last year, if ye'll recall. Home a short time and away again," she added with a wave of her hand. She tilted her head and fixed her gaze on Fenella to emphasize her words. Or was she trying to imply something?

"Aye, I do recall it," Fenella confirmed, refusing to take her friend's bait. The laird had sent his heir to negotiate with a distant clan to trade lambs for grain. The travel alone would have taken weeks, much less the time spent in talks with the other laird. Keenan had returned home for a few weeks, then been sent out again to treat with another clan.

Her friend, like most people in the village, not just the women, loved gossip. Most events didn't have a town crier like the lad spreading the news. The local busybodies took care of that. Her friend was not usually one of them, so Fenella wondered why this interested her so. But if she asked, she'd be here for hours yet, and she couldn't stay much longer. "Perhaps this bairn is simply waiting for its da to return yet again."

"How would it ken when its da is due home?"

Fenella chuckled at that. The weaver had a sharp sense of humor, but she was right. "No bairn would, of course," she demurred. "And for that matter, no one in the clan kens when Keenan and his men will return from his latest journey." Perhaps it would be today. Perhaps next month. Perhaps, if the worst happened, never.

She shook her head, willing away that thought. Keenan was Gavan's eldest brother. Her Gavan. The man she expected to marry.

"Still missing yer lad, are ye?"

Fenella sighed. "Ye ken me too well."

The man she was waiting for had been away for months, traveling on the continent or who knew where. She'd hoped to be wedded by now, but there'd been no word of him. Or from him. No letters home. Nothing to let the clan—or her—know where he was or what he was doing. Or when to expect him. In that way, he was much like his eldest brother. Would Gavan ever settle down—with her?

"As much as the frustration of not knowing about Gavan is eating away at me, I can only imagine how hard the waiting has to be for Aimil. She must be frantic with wanting Keenan with her when the bairn comes."

Fenella's situation was not the same. She and Gavan had an understanding between them before he left, but not a formal betrothal. He refused to bind her to him when he didn't know what his future held. So she waited and fumed, envious of Keenan's and Aimil's certainty. Their marriage and happiness. Their bairn, now finally about to arrive.

As a young lass, Fenella had once dreamed of becoming Keenan's wife, but as she grew, she came to understand the responsibility borne by the heir to the clan. Aimil was a MacKinnon, married into MacNabb for the alliance and the dowry she brought. Fenella had accepted he would never be hers.

She felt cheated by fate, and yet, she knew she should not. She'd been given a good home, accepted as a MacNabb. But as the Leny chief's daughter, she would have married well with an heir such as Keenan, not a third son like Gavan. She'd have been a lady.

Nay, that wasn't fair. She had not settled for a third son. Gavan was a wonderful man, strong, handsome, accomplished, who cared for her and her alone. She would be proud to be his wife and satisfied to make a family with him. She would not be the lady of the clan, but someday, as the laird's brother, Gavan would hold an honored position in the clan, and so would she.

That was important to her. She'd come to the clan a wee orphan. Her father was the chief of Leny, a MacMillan sept. Both her parents had been killed in clan wars that little by little had wiped out her family line. The new chief, a distant cousin far removed from the conflict, had sent her to the closest clan that would take her in as a future bride to one of their lads, one of several Leny orphans scattered among the highland clans. She would have been important to Leny in the way Keenan's wife was to his, had her family survived.

The weaver crossed her arms and shuddered. "I canna imagine. Nor do I want to. We can only wish her well."

"Aye, and pray for both of them."

"For her and the bairn?"

"For her and Keenan. He must return soon." For all to be well, he needed to be at home. Could prayers reach him and hurry him on his way? No matter the mission for their clan that called him away, he was needed here.

The sound of horse's hooves clattering through the village disturbed her ruminations. "What is happening?"

The weaver stood and went to the door. "Ye willna believe it, but Keenan is back. He and all his men are home." She turned away from the door, a broad smile lighting her face. "He is in time to see his bairn arrive. Perhaps the bairn did ken its da was near."

"Surely ye didna believe me. I was jesting." Still, Aimil

would have the comfort of her husband as their bairn arrived, so fortune had provided what was needed. Fenella's vigil for Gavan would have to go on.

"Why no'? It makes as much sense as any other reason I can think of."

Keenan was home, but the weaver had not mentioned Gavan. Well, she had no reason to think fortune would have smiled on the brothers such that they would have crossed paths and brought them both home together.

Fenella forced herself to return her friend's smile, then stood. "I should get back to the keep. The family will be in an uproar. 'Twill be good to see their happiness, twice over, this day." And perhaps, someday soon, Gavan would arrive as Keenan had, all unexpected but welcomed.

"Go on with ye, then," the weaver told her. "Enjoy the celebration. I'll be along later."

Fenella made the short walk to the keep so quickly, Keenan and his men were still in the bailey, stable lads taking charge of their horses after the men stripped saddle bags and other belongings from them. The laird and lady waited on the keep's steps for their son to approach them. Fenella waited with others of the clan watching the return until Keenan greeted his parents and followed them inside. Still part of the throng, she entered the great hall, where food and drink were being set out on long trestle tables for the midday meal. Some seated near the hearth murmured prayers, as did others scattered through the hall.

Keenan had disappeared, either to his father's solar, or to his wife's childbed, Fenella didn't know. Which would he deem most important? To report to his father or to support his wife in her labor?

Her friend, Groa, approached her, smiling. "What perfect timing! Trust my brother to arrive just as his bairn makes ready to join us."

"Being heir does bring some benefits, I suppose," Fenella told her with a grin. "To be capable of such perfect timing, I mean. How goes Aimil's confinement?"

"Well enough, it seems. This bairn willna be rushed."

"Poor Aimil."

"Aye, and poor Keenan, to have to wait through it all. But it serves him right for all the time she has had to spend awaiting his return."

"Is he with her?"

Groa nodded toward her brother, just leaving the laird's solar and making his way through the crowded hall toward the stairs. "He is on his way. Da had to have his few minutes with him as laird to heir before releasing him to be a husband, and soon, a father."

Fenella crossed her arms as she watched Keenan mount the stairs. "So much responsibility."

"Aye, and my brother will carry it well. Of that, I have nay doubt."

Fenella had to agree with her. The laird was already turning over many of his own tasks to his heir. Keenan would be well-prepared before his time came to assume leadership of MacNabb, which, God willing, would not be for years.

"I suppose ye've yet to hear from my wayward middle brother," Groa said with a twist of her lips.

"Neither have ye or ye wouldna ask," Fenella said with a shrug, though the question made her belly clench with unlooked-for resentment. "He's either too busy to write or—"

"Or many things. Dinna borrow trouble, my friend. Especially not on this day."

Fenella shook her head. "'Twas nay my intent. I meant only to say that couriers may be scarce wherever he has wandered."

A sudden shriek from above stairs silenced the crowd in the great hall. Another followed.

"Things are progressing," Groa muttered, wincing in sympathy.

Fenella didn't respond, her gaze on the stairs, but her heart in her throat. What would the rest of this day bring? The joy of a successful childbirth to add to the well-timed arrival of its father? Or more waiting? She refused to consider anything else.

Intermittent cries continued for the rest of the after-noon and into the evening, becoming fainter and farther apart. The mood in the great hall had gone from jubilant to wary, mirroring Fenella's own. Most traded worried glances as the sound of their muttered prayers rose and fell. No one could doubt Aimil was exhausted by her labor. How much longer could she continue?

Silence disturbed only by praying went another hour into the night before an infant's wail sounded, breaking the somber mood that had settled over the hall like a low cloud. A collective gasp filled the hall, then laughter and cheers broke out. The bairn had arrived and lived! Fenella joined in the laughter, relief making her as giddy as the others in the hall. This was a day of joy indeed.

Before long, one of the healer's apprentices appeared on the upstairs landing and the crowd quieted to hear her announcement.

"A lass is born," she said, then retreated from view.

Fenella thought it odd that she showed no great enthusiasm, no smile, no excitement over the new bairn. Nor did she present the wee lass. But perhaps she had been with the healer during most of the day and was as tired as everyone in the birthing chamber must be.

"Ah, da will be disappointed 'tis nay a son and heir," Groa said, still sitting at Fenella's side after the long hours spent waiting. "But happy, too."

Had Groa noticed the lass's solemn tone? "Aye, we lasses have our uses," Fenella retorted, relief and weariness suddenly making her snappish. Perhaps in her fatigue, she'd imagined the subdued tone.

Groa nodded but didn't take the bait. "Where is Keenan? I wonder why he didna bring out his daughter."

"Holding her mother's hand, or I miss my guess," Fenella told her, reaching for an explanation that made sense. "I daresay he didna want to leave her side, or to relinquish the bairn, if only long enough to show her to the clan."

Groa put a hand on Fenella's arm. "Ah, there go da and mother," she said, pointing to her parents ascending the stairs. "Time for the family to invade, I suppose," she added and stood. "Want to come see the wee lass?"

Suddenly reluctant, Fenella shook her head. "Ye go. 'Tis meant to be family time. Keenan will want ye there. I'll have plenty of chances later."

Groa took her arm. "Nay, ye are part of the family—or someday will be. Ye dinna want to miss yer future niece's first breaths. Come with me."

Fenella nodded, still reluctant but unwilling to make a scene with her friend at such a time as this. She appreciated Groa including her in the family, but she was only being kind. Fenella's future was very much in doubt as long as Gavan stayed away. She couldn't be certain of her welcome in the birthing room. Would she be treated as an interloper, even though Groa brought her? She hoped not. Torn, she moved with Groa across the great hall and followed her up the stairs.

The first thing she noticed as Groa opened the door and they entered the room was the heat and the smell. The flames of many candles added to the heat of so many people in the chamber. Keenan's parents and two of his brothers, Gregor and Donal, the healer's apprentice, and herself and Groa in addition to the new parents and the infant filled the space. Blood and other things Fenella was in no hurry to name assaulted her nose, sharp and cloying and thick.

No one was moving. They stood around the bed, watching Keenan kneel by his wife, the babe at her pale breast but not suckling. Then Fenella understood what was happening and turned for the door.

Groa's hand shot out and grabbed her wrist, the expression on her face a silent plea not to leave her. Fenella nodded and put her other hand over her friend's, offering what little comfort she could.

Aimil lay dying.

Keenan hunched over her, stroking her sweat-soaked hair with one hand, the other on his daughter's back. Tears dripped unheeded onto his wife's neck and shoulder, both so pale as to be almost blue.

Fenella's gaze swept the room and she understood the reason for the strong scent of blood. In bringing her daughter into the world, Aimil had bled, heavily. The healer had been unable to stop it.

The healer! Where was she? Irritation pierced Fenella's dismay and she turned to glance out the door behind her, but the woman was not there, either. The healer should still be here, trying to save her dying patient.

After a few more agonized moments, Aimil gave a

shuddering exhale, then breathed no more. No one moved, but at Fenella's side, Groa gave a small cry of protest.

Keenan dropped his forehead to his wife's, then kissed her lightly on the lips.

"My poor son," his mother murmured, her gaze on Keenan and the dead woman.

The infant started crying, soon escalating to hacking wails.

"Groa, where is the healer? Yer niece needs a wet nurse," Fenella said softly. "Now," she said, adding urgency to her tone, "or ye'll lose the wee one, too."

Groa seemed in shock, as did her parents and Keenan's brothers. Fenella couldn't stand it. Someone had to do something to quiet the bairn. To help her. She moved forward and picked up the wee lass from her mother's body, cradling her against her chest.

"Where did the healer go?" Fenella may as well have said nothing. No one answered, so she grabbed a plaid from a chair near the door, laid it over the infant and left the room. At the top of the stairs, she showed the lass. "Is there a wet nurse in the clan? Any woman willing to suckle the heir's babe along with her own? Her mother canna do it."

"I will," one lass said. "I still have milk enough."

Fenella went down the stairs to her, careful to keep one hand on the railing. She dared not fall with the newborn in her arms.

"Ah, good, ye have kept her warm," the lass said as she reached for the babe and pulled aside her shift. In moments, the bairn had latched on and was feeding, if slowly. "She'll take more as she gets stronger," the lass said.

Fenella nodded. "Thank ye. I dinna ken yer name."

"I'm from another village, visiting a friend. I'm Mara."

"Fenella. I must find someone in the village who can become the nurse for this lass."

Another woman came up to them. "My daughter Kyla can serve," she said. "My other daughter can care for her young son for now. He's old enough to cease nursing."

Relief filled Fenella. With the help of the village, she hoped the new bairn might live, and Keenan would not have to bury her, too, with her mother.

"Has anyone seen the healer?"

"Aye, she went to her herbal some time ago," one of the men sitting nearby said.

"Come with me," Fenella said to Mara. "If ye can? The healer should see this wee one."

Later, fed and sound asleep, the bairn stayed in Fenella's arms as she, Mara and the local lass, Kyla, proceeded to the nursery. The healer, who had still looked shaken and sad, had pronounced the wee one well and strong, "Settle in here for tonight, please," Fenella told the lasses. "I'm certain the family will be grateful for yer help. Ye will see them on the morrow."

Mara settled in a chair. Fenella gave the wee bairn into

her arms, and a sweet smile lit Mara's face as she gazed down at her.

Despite the tragedy that had brought them here, Fenella couldn't help the small flare of jealousy as she gazed at the bairn's sweet face in Mara's arms. When would her turn come to marry and have bairns of her own? Or would she wind up like Aimil? She looked away from the bairn, fighting to keep her last memory of the wee one's poor mother out of her mind. As a chill slithered down her spine, she left the nursery, went down the stair and through the great hall, needing to be away from the sadness that overlay the miracle of this new life. She pushed open the keep's heavy door and left the crowded hall for some air in the bailey. The night was clear and cold. Stars seemed to be bright shards of crystal so thick, they appeared like clouds against the black sky. They should name the lass Astra, Fenella thought. For a night with so many stars they nearly hid the dark. Nearly, but not quite. And the full moon would rise late and hang in the morning sky like a wraith.

Fenella shivered and turned to reenter the keep, leaving that image outside. It had no place in the hall this night.

She went back to the birthing chamber in time for Keenan to step out of the door, his wife's body wrapped in a blood-soaked sheet in his arms. His mother noticed her and stopped him.

"Ye took the wee lass. Where is she?"

"In the nursery with two wet nurses for tonight. Tomorrow, ye may wish to make yer own arrangements for her."

That got her a wan smile. "Thank ye for doing what we should have. The shock..."

Fenella looked from her to the woman in Keenan's arms and finally to him. His face showed no expression, but his eyes gave away the agony that must be clawing at his insides. How did he bear it? "I understand. The healer waits for ye. I'm so sorry."

She stepped out of the way and they continued to the top of the stairs. All conversation in the great hall died the moment they appeared. She was certain Keenan didn't notice the sudden hush as he took his wife to be prepared for burial.

Fenella had no doubt servants were already in the birthing chamber, cleaning it. Tomorrow, it would be as if tonight had never happened, except for the missing woman and the new bairn. The thought gave her a strange hollow sense in the pit of her stomach. Nothing was the same, and would never be the same again.

———

THE DAY AFTER THE NEXT, THE MORNING WAS DARK, THE waning moon invisible above low clouds and heavy rain.

Cold wind whistled across the rushing burn that bordered the rise in the glen where Keenan MacNabb's family had long buried their dead. Fenella's gaze strayed from the simple wooden box holding the remains of Keenan's late wife to the babe in Kyla's arms, the village lass who'd become her wet nurse, and to Keenan, stone-faced, gaze downcast as four strong men of the clan lowered his dead wife's body into the muddy ground. She would find it a boggy place to rest. Fenella had no doubt that rainwater had started to fill the hole. She hoped Aimil's soul ascended quickly on the words of the priest commending her to God, if it hadn't already, and spared her that knowledge.

The infant she'd died to bring into the world started to cry, as if she knew her mother was gone and she would never see her again. Never feel her touch. Never get to know the love between her parents that had brought her into being. Fenella's heart broke for the wee bairn and for its father, who faced the loss of all the dreams they'd shared, and instead, now faced raising a daughter without her mother.

But he had his clan and this village. Judging from some of the glances traded among the unattached lasses, he'd have more help, and more consoling, than any one man could possibly need.

Those lasses glanced her way with speculation in their eyes. Did they think if one brother failed to claim her, the other would do? The elder? The future laird? She pursed her lips, hating how the notion raised a flare of hope in her chest. Hope and something more—ambition? With time, could Keenan come to see her as something other than Gavan's intended?

The idea saddened Fenella even further. She didn't know if the man she'd promised to wait for, Keenan's younger brother, was still alive, or how he would come to know of his brother's loss. Or if he would ever return to claim her.

Nay. She couldn't dwell on such an idea. She'd be no better than these grasping lasses, eyeing Keenan before his dead wife was covered up in the cold, muddy ground.

But her daughter—

As the infant wailed in protest of the cold and wet, Fenella saw an honorable way to support Keenan and keep herself allied with his family until Gavan returned—which he would do. She could not let herself imagine anything else. Gavan would come home. Eventually. Hopefully before he forgot her, and before she wasted her youth, or her life, waiting for him. She would ensure a place for herself with his family, so that when he did return, she would have their support while the promise Gavan and she had made to each other sustained them until they became reacquainted.

Keenan dropped a handful of earth onto the casket, then turned away. His shoulders rounded as though he fought the need to bend double with grief and pain. Then he straightened and trudged toward the wee bridge over the burn and the path that led to the gates of the MacNabb keep, his sister Groa keeping pace silently at his side, his brothers following and their parents walking slowly a few steps behind their children. He never looked back.

His daughter's cries didn't stop him or change the path he walked. The nameless lass. Keenan was too grief stricken to name her and others would not do so until she reached several months of age. Any child might die all too easily, but a motherless child was more at risk. Better to let her go, if that was to be her fate, without a name to keep in the hearts of those who wanted to love her. Or hate her for the death of her mother. Would Keenan hate his daughter? The thought soured in her belly. How could he? The bairn was all that was left of his wife.

Fenella did not hold with the superstition that denied this bairn a name. Yet it was not her place to name Keenan's daughter, or even to encourage him to do so. Perhaps if she could care for her well enough, if he saw her thrive, he would claim her and bestow whatever name he or her mother had decided to give her. Fenella swore to do what little she could to ensure that happened.

She fought back the tears that had mixed with rain-drops on her face, and resolved, strode to the wet nurse, who was frantically trying to soothe her charge and silence her. Fenella took the infant from Kyla's arms, and rocked her. Her cries calmed and her eyes closed, leaving tears to dry on her tiny face.

Fenella walked through the keep's gates with the bairn

on her shoulder, the wet nurse trudging behind her through the muddy ground. She nodded to the bairn's grandmother, the clan's lady, who gave her a sad smile and permitted her to continue without questioning why she had the bairn and not the woman following her. Her approval gave Fenella hope that when Gavan returned, they could start where they left off, and not as the strangers they might have become. His family, accustomed to her presence with the wee lass, would accept her as his.

She stayed in the nursery and warmed herself at its hearth fire while the wet nurse fed the wee lass. The midday meal would be a solemn affair at best. She'd rather remain with the infant than endure the gloom that would inhabit the great hall. Here, at least, was new life, and hope for a future, even if it was different than the future anyone in the clan, especially Keenan, had envisioned.

But she couldn't hide, any more than he could. His family would see him through the meal, and so must she, if she was to retain the ground she'd gained with his mother. She nodded to Kyla, then stood and left her suckling the bairn.

The great hall was as silent and still as Fenella had expected. She took a seat within view of the upper table, but not so close as to appear presumptuous or, like some of the other lasses, determined to be noticed by Keenan. Rather, she found a place below the side where his mother sat, solemn and picking at the food on her trencher.

It hurt Fenella to watch her. As soon as Keenan left, his

parents stood to go. Fenella took that as permission for everyone else to do the same. Groa stood at the same time and raised a hand to halt her, then came down from the dais to meet her.

"Thank ye for taking care of the wee bairn," Groa told her. "I saw how she responded to ye. Ye are good for her and I hope ye will find it within ye to spend more time with her."

"Of course," Fenella promised, shocked at the notice Groa gave her during such a grievous time.

"My brother is too wounded right now to give his daughter the care she needs, and frankly, a woman's touch is better for her, I think."

"But Keenan needs his daughter, too."

"He will, but not today. Perhaps not this sennight. He must come to terms with what has happened and what is left to him. An infant daughter isna something he ever thought to be responsible for on his own."

"He willna be alone in this."

"Ye?" The look Groa gave her was speculative rather than censoring.

Fenella shook her head. "Nay, 'tis no' what I meant. He has ye. His family. People who love him and care for him."

Groa nodded. "Ye are right. 'Tis too soon by far for another lass to enter his heart. It still bleeds. I ken ye and Gavan cared for each other—and may still do so despite his long absence. But I thank ye for anything ye are willing to do to help us ease Keenan's burden, and to keep his daughter well until he can accept her."

Fenella nodded, throat so tight, she found herself unable to speak.

Groa took her hand and squeezed it, then left her standing in the middle of the hall fighting for calm, overwhelmed by the responsibility Keenan's sister had laid upon her, despite her earlier resolve to do just what Groa had suggested.

———

AS THE MONTHS WENT BY, THE WEE LASS, STILL NAMELESS, grew strong and thrived. Her father did not fare as well. The grief that consumed him at his wife's sudden death had not eased its grip. He continued with his responsibilities as his father's heir, and in the company of other men seemed to come back to himself, though he remained mostly silent and closed off, avoiding many of the women of the clan, especially if they resembled his dead wife.

With regret and no small measure of reluctance, Fenella had given up on Gavan ever returning. She spent as much time with Keenan's daughter as she could, and even brought the wee lass to her father. He would hold her, but seemed lost in thought, not really present with her, even when she cried. Fenella would take her from him when that happened, fearing her cries would upset him, but in asking silent permission to do so, would touch

Keenan's shoulder and place a sympathetic hand there. Only then did he seem to come back to the present, look up and actually see her. Lately, he placed his hand over hers on his shoulder, making Fenella's heart race with surprise and pleasure that he'd acknowledged her touch.

Groa, present during several of these instances, watched closely. Once they were away from Keenan, she said, "ye are the only lass he seems to respond to, save me and mother. Have ye noticed?"

"Nay. Ye are mistaken. He's finally responding to the bairn."

Groa shook her head. "Nay, 'tis more than that. Ye are helping the father as well as the daughter. The ice in his heart is starting to melt. And when it does, I would be proud to call ye sister and someday, Lady MacNabb."

Astounded, Fenella said the first thing that popped into her head. "Gavan—"

"Has been gone so long he may have married another, or, well, I dinna wish to dwell on other possibilities to explain his absence. The two of ye were too young to understand that love and marriage are built on respect and trust and responsibility for each other. Keenan is here. Now. And he sees only ye. Think on that."

"I...Groa, ye ken what the clan will say. That I have traded one brother for another. I'll be seen as nay better than any of the lasses who've tried to trip him into their beds these last months."

"They willna. The family will make sure ye are seen as

the reason his daughter still lives, and that he is coming back to himself and to us. Ye must consider my words. I dinna ken what will happen if ye were to back away from him now."

Fenella did hear her. Groa's words shocked her, yet the more she considered them, the more the idea appealed. Keenan would come back to himself. She would continue to help him. His daughter needed him. The clan needed him.

Perhaps, given Gavan's long absence and lack of contact with her or anyone else in his family, so did she. Keenan had given her a place to fit in, to be accepted, and to be useful, whether he intended to or not. Whether he realized it or not. Perhaps now, it was up to her to make him see how the change Groa claimed she'd wrought in him had also changed her. And how the two of them, nay, the three with his daughter, could go forward together and make a real home and family. And someday, perhaps, fall in love.

The next time she and Groa attended Keenan with his daughter, when the bairn began to cry, Groa stepped forward and took her from her brother. "I'll take her to the wet nurse," Groa announced and left them alone.

Fenella knew what she was up to, but she went along with it, hoping to see what effect she might have on Keenan in private. When he lifted his gaze to meet hers and the corners of his lips quivered upward, she held back a gasp and gave him a small smile of her own.

"Thank ye," he said, his voice soft, almost too low to hear.

"For what? I've done naught—"

"Ye've done more than ye ken, Fenella. I heard what ye did the night Aimil..." He choked to a stop and took a breath, then continued. "Ye have saved my wee lass and given me the time I needed with her to...to—"

She put a hand on his shoulder. It was the only touch she was accustomed to giving him, but she felt he needed it, perhaps nearly as much as she did in this moment. "Dinna say it, Keenan. Yer family, the whole clan, have done what they can to help ye. Ye are getting better. I see it. Groa sees it. I hope ye see it, too."

He reached up and covered her hand with his own, then smiled again, softly, but this time a touch ruefully. "I do. 'Tis past time for me to begin to live again. To care for my daughter—with yer help and that of my family. I've let grief consume me for too long."

"Or just long enough to let yer heart begin to heal," Fenella assured him as he squeezed her hand and let his drop away.

His gaze shifted to the far distance. "I canna see her face any longer." He met her gaze, and the pain in his eyes made her chest ache. "What if I forget her? I never want to."

"Ye willna," she told him as firmly as she could around the lump in her throat. "She will always be part of ye. As she should. Yer time together may have been too short, but she gave ye the greatest gift before she left ye. Ye will see her again in yer daughter as she grows into a young woman."

He nodded; his gaze lost again in a distance only he could see.

Fenella allowed herself to hope, without guilt, that his distant vision included her.

HEART OF HOPE

This story follows my Highland Talents series prequel, HEART OF STONE. If you haven't read it, or haven't read it in a while, now would be a great time to put a bookmark here and go read it. Then continue with this story, and you'll have the arc of Keenan and Fenella's love match brought to a satisfying end.

In this story, though a wedding is expected, the road to true love never does run smoothly, or, sometimes, at all. But there will be a happy ending!

It's a romance, after all.

SCOTTISH HIGHLANDS, AUTUMN 1502

"I thought this day would never come," Fenella MacNabb confided to Gavan as she smoothed the skirt of the dress she would soon be married in.

"And I never doubted that it would," he told her. She lifted a hand and he adjusted the polished steel tray that served as a mirror to show her more of her reflection. "Ye mean too much to the clan for this wedding no' to take place," he added.

"That means more to me than ye ken, especially coming from ye," she told him, looking at him rather than her blurry image. She appreciated the sentiment, and that it came from Gavan. "I'm glad to have ye as a brother," she added, hand over her heart. "And that we were able to settle our differences these long months past." Then she nodded for him to put the tray aside.

"I am, too. Ye have been so good for Keenan. Ye have

cared for Máirín and for her father for more than a year. 'Tis time to tie the knot."

"He needed someone." She paused as Gavan crossed his arms and gave her a stern look, brows lowered. "Verra well, he needed me. And I am honored to be the one he chose." She gave him a knowing smile. "Marsali has been good for ye, too."

A knock at the door announced Marsali's arrival, her favorite deerhound Corrie on her heels. "Ye sent for me? Ah, Fenella, look at ye! Ye look wonderful! I love the embroidery ye added to the neckline of your kirtle. Ah, look! Are those bluebells? Corrie, sit down over there. Fenella doesna need yer hair on her dress."

"They are," Fenella answered, grateful for Marsali's thoughtfulness and Corrie's obedience. "The bluebells represent ye, of course. I chose a flower or plant for each member of the family. I'm glad ye like it."

"I dinna like it. I love it. And so will Lady MacNabb. Ye ken how sentimental she is about family."

"Fenella was just telling me how glad she is to have me as a brother," Gavan told Marsali with a grin.

"Me, too," Marsali replied. "That he has ye for a sister, I mean, as well as a friend."

Fenella grinned with them. Marsali knew their history. She'd had her nose rubbed in it when she first arrived at MacNabb with him. But she'd learned that Fenella was Gavan's past, and that Marsali was the only future he wanted. She wasn't jealous of the friendship they'd managed to retain through it all.

"Keenan is pacing in the bailey," Marsali warned. "But he canna stop smiling."

Fenella laughed, grateful for Marsali's attempt to keep her mood light.

Gavan and Marsali had married months before, not long after he'd encountered her near her home in the moonlight in a ring of standing stones. She'd woven a love spell with a chain of bluebells that at first seemed not to work, but the spell and her deerhound Corrie seemed to conspire to bring them together—with some help from both their fathers.

Fenella, in the years Gavan had been away from the clan, had fallen for Keenan and his motherless daughter, Máirín. Caring for the babe led to caring for its father, and eventually brought Keenan out of the cloud of grief over his wife's sudden death that threatened to choke the life from him as well.

Now they were to be married. Fenella fought to contain her excitement and appear serene as they headed outdoors to the kirk steps, where by now Keenan would be waiting.

He greeted her with a chaste kiss on her cheek and took her hand. "Ye are always beautiful, my love," he told her, "but especially today."

"I am proud to become yer wife," she said softly. "I love ye and ye ken I love Máirín, too."

He nodded. "Perhaps more than ye love me."

Fenella didn't know what to say to that. His tone sounded serious, but he might be jesting, something he did so rarely, she might fail to recognize it. He saved her from a reply by turning her to face the priest. It was finally happening! She was marrying the man who had stolen her heart. She would be mother in truth to Máirín, the bairn she had raised from the day she was born from her dying mother's womb.

She glanced aside. Keenan appeared calm, which was usual for him now that the worst of the fog of grief had finally left him. He was not given to displays of emotion. But he turned his head to her and smiled, lifting her heart. From any other man, that would seem faint praise, but from him, she knew he meant to tell her how overjoyed he was to be standing here with her.

The day could not be more perfect for their union to be solemnized, and for the clan to accept her as their future Lady. All her hopes and dreams, all her ambitions as a woman, a wife, and someone the clan looked up to, depended on this one, simple act. Marrying this man, caring for his daughter, and someday, she hoped, giving him a male heir to carry forward the MacNabb name, were everything to her.

While the priest spoke the words that would make her Keenan's wife and he, her husband, her awareness stayed on the man at her side. The back of his hand brushed hers, silently lending her a portion of his strength.

When the priest finished speaking, he turned to

Keenan's father for the length of MacNabb plaid to bind their hands together in the first part of the ceremony.

The old laird's face reddened, and he gasped. He reached out to the priest as if handing him the cloth, then dropped to his knees and clutched his chest.

"Da!" Keenan's cry broke the frozen stillness that gripped everyone as the laird fell. Gasps and cries of concern filled the air as Keenan knelt to lift his father to his feet. But the old laird's eyes widened, then closed, and he collapsed into Keenan's arms. Fenella reached out to aid him, but Keenan's brothers gathered around him and helped him lay their father down on the step above where they were standing. The healer rushed forward and shooed the men out of her way. In moments, she stood and shook her head, her gaze downcast.

"The laird is dead," she said quietly to his sons.

Fenella clenched her hands over her heart. This could not be happening.

"Do something!" Keenan demanded.

Fenella's heart broke for the desperation in his voice. First his wife died suddenly at a time that should have been filled with joy, and now his father had done the same.

The healer shook her head again. "He's gone, Laird MacNabb."

Keenan stepped back, wide-eyed shock on his face as he registered her use of the title that, all his life, had belonged to his father.

The priest began last rites there on the steps. Keenan

found his voice enough to tell his brothers to carry the old laird into the kirk for his last rites. They obeyed, walking slowly up the center aisle, their mother following them and her husband's body, her steps painfully slow, her head bowed, but her back straight and stiff until she took the seat in the first pew that the priest directed her to. Lacking a coffin, his sons laid him in front of the altar on the cold stone floor.

Keenan watched from outside, breathing deeply. He had disappeared into the numbness tightening his jaw and shoulders. Fenella had seen him do this before when he tried his hardest to gather himself. He needed that calm control now more than ever.

Of course, he hadn't expected to hear the title addressed to him. Not today. Fenella reached for him, putting a comforting hand on his arm.

But he shrugged her off. "Stay here."

Dismayed by his rejection, Fenella obeyed.

The priest's sonorous voice echoed in the nearly empty kirk. The clan gathered for a wedding now clustered on the steps to observe the priest's ritual. She'd been moments away from becoming Keenan's wife, and now she was relegated to remaining outside while the family went in. Her heart had broken for the laird's family, but it broke yet again for her dashed hopes and dreams while Keenan turned away from her and walked slowly up the center aisle past benches on either side. He joined his brothers in standing over their father's body until the priest finished.

As one, his brothers turned to Keenan and knelt. One-by-one, they swore fealty to the new laird MacNabb. Gavan went first. He was paler than she'd ever seen him, and his jaw clenched again and again as he spoke the ritual words. Anyone who didn't know him might think he objected to the oath he gave, but she knew better. Keenan's brothers idolized him and expected him to be a worthy successor to their da. Gregor went next, and Donal last. Pale and shaking, Donal knelt on one knee beside his father's still warm body and kept glancing at it as he spoke. He'd returned to MacNabb from his new home at Clan Lathan to celebrate his eldest brother's wedding. Their sister Groa remained there, wed to a Lathan and unable to travel due to her first pregnancy. Their two youngest brothers were fostered away and had not been summoned to attend today. Fenella had been sad Groa would miss her wedding. Now, she could only be relieved that her friend would not have to endure witnessing this tragedy unfold.

Keenan stood, silent and stoic while he accepted his brothers' oaths, then clasped each one on the shoulder and thanked them for their faith in him.

Fenella sank onto a bench at the back of the kirk. Watching Keenan set the tone for the clan in the midst of such tragedy, the pieces of her heart shattered yet again for him.

Oath-taking done, he folded his mother in his arms and held her, letting her tears soak his leine until she pulled out of his grasp and dropped to her knees by her husband.

She took his hand. "My laird," she said. "My love," she added, more softly. "How cruel the way ye chose to leave us." She kissed his hand, then stood with Keenan's help and turned to regard him and the priest. "We came for a wedding. Ye must complete that. My son needs a strong woman at his side, especially now."

Fenella stood, expecting the priest to invite her to stand by her betrothed or to move Keenan to her rather than marry them over his father's body. But Keenan hesitated, and she held her breath.

Would Keenan still want her? His father had allowed their marriage within MacNabb since his heir had wed once before, to Aimil, to cement an alliance with McKinnon. Would Keenan's sudden duty as laird convince him that alliances were more important than their feelings for each other, especially if alliances had not been made or refreshed with powerful neighbors in a long time?

"Nay, Mother," Keenan said, holding up a hand when the priest opened his mouth to agree to proceed. He squared his shoulders. "Our allies must be advised. We will bury our laird first. The wedding will wait for a more auspicious day." He turned his head and looked toward Fenella, his gaze remote, as if he didn't really see her.

She had her answer. Keenan might always associate the idea of their wedding with his father's death. If so, the future she'd dreamed of and aspired to was doomed. That auspicious day might never come, not for her. Everyone knew alerting the clan's allies would bring a flood of condolences—and offers to renew alliances through marriage.

She felt eyes boring into her back and glanced around. The people outside the kirk clogged the doorway, the crowd ebbing and flowing as each person shifted for a view of the people inside, including her. Were their eyes filled with pity? Or satisfaction? She dared not look at them for long or they would focus on her instead of their new laird. He was important to the clan. She was not.

Silently, she cursed the old laird for his timing. Yet in her heart, she knew he would not have chosen this manner of death, nor this time.

———

Two days later, after the sun rose above the nearby hills, they laid the old laird in the ground. The clan gathered for the ceremony and to observe the ritual. The priest officiated. The widow and the new MacNabb laird and his brothers threw the first earth on the casket. Fenella hung back as the rest of the clan stepped forward to do the same, no longer feeling a part of the family. She'd come so close. Moments only from being, at least, hand fasted, and minutes from being married in the kirk and acclaimed by the clan.

Keenan had not spoken to her since his father collapsed.

It wasn't fair. She held his daughter, even now, little more regarded than a wet nurse, the recipient of sorrowful, sympathetic glances from some of the women, and snide, haughty smirks from others.

It didn't take long after the burial for word of the change of leadership at MacNabb to bring messengers with offers of alliance and of marriage to eligible daughters. The first arrived two days later, but after a week, they still arrived. Each time she heard hoofbeats approaching MacNabb's gates, Fenella's heart clenched. Keenan would be closeted for hours with each messenger, and then with his advisors. She dreaded the news to come, but she fully expected she'd soon hear that he'd chosen a mate from among those being offered.

She still cared for Máirín. How could she not? She was the only mother the lass had ever known. Máirín seemed most to enjoy being outside, Fenella strolling the glen and the trees near the keep's walls with the bairn in her arms. Máirín would laugh as leaf shadows slipped over Fenella's face, and reach for the tears that slid down her cheeks when, away from other people, she gave in to her misery.

Returning to the keep after a walk outside, Fenella took Máirín back to the nursery.

"Have ye heard?" Kyla asked as Fenella turned away. She seemed bursting to tell her something.

Fenella looked over her shoulder. "Heard what?"

"The Cameron offered a fabulous dowry for the laird to marry his youngest daughter. MacNabb will be wealthy! 'Tis said the lass is only nine years old, so 'twould be years before the laird could get an heir on her, but 'twould be worth the wait. His mother could remain chatelaine and train up the lass until she bled."

Fenella's stomach lurched. She managed to say, "I hadna heard," before she fled the nursery for her own chamber. There, she was sick again and again until there was nothing left in her belly save sour tears. Her fears were coming true. Keenan would never be hers. And she couldn't bear to see him wed to anyone else, to watch their love bloom and their bairns born.

She would have to leave MacNabb. But where? The only alternative she could think of was that perhaps Marsali's Murray clan would welcome her.

Fenella dreaded that night's supper, expecting to hear that Keenan was going to accept the Cameron offer. But she couldn't tolerate being ignored any longer, so when she happened upon him in the hallway, she stopped him with a hand on his arm. "Can ye nay look at me, Keenan? I'm the woman ye claimed to love and were going to marry. Is it more than ye can manage to speak to me? To tell me what ye are planning? For yer daughter's sake at least?"

He squeezed his eyes shut, giving her hope that he'd realize how badly he'd hurt her, and give her something to cling to. But he only shook his head, removed her hand from his arm with his free hand, and went on his way.

Shocked, Fenella stood, barely breathing. She hadn't expected he would continue to ignore her if she confronted him. Worse, the warmth of his hand on hers had sent hot shivers up her arm, reminding her how she loved his touch. He paused a dozen steps away and for a heart-rending moment, she believed he would turn back to her, but he continued on.

He made no announcement during the meal.

She picked at her food, and left as soon as others began to leave the hall. After their encounter, Keenan's disregard for her during the meal had been the last arrow her heart could absorb.

She sought out Marsali. "I need yer help," she told her when they adjourned to Fenella's chamber. "Ye must have seen that Keenan refuses to notice me, even when I care for his daughter. And ye must have heard the rumors of great wealth being offered MacNabb in dowries."

"I'm so sorry, Fenella," Marsali told her. "What can I do?"

"Tell me how to get to Murray. And that yer da—and yer clan—would welcome me. I canna remain here and watch Keenan wed another. I canna! But I dinna ken where to go. Or how to leave Máirín behind. But I must."

She fought back tears, but lost the battle when Marsali put an arm around her shoulders.

"'Tis really that bad?"

"'Tis worse," Fenella replied, choking back a sob and breathing hard to get control of herself. She was stronger than this. "I'm sorry," she said once she could speak.

"Ye have naught to be sorry for. Ye have been good for both of them. And ye were about to be married. None of this is yer fault. I dinna ken what Keenan is thinking. What he's doing." Marsali released her and stepped back, determination in her eyes. "But I will ask Gavan what is going on. Perhaps ye are wrong, and Keenan is simply dealing with suddenly becoming laird. When he gains his stride, he will return to ye."

"Nay, I dinna think he will. He refuses to see me. Not even in passing. He hasna spoken a word to me since that day on the kirk steps. He willna meet my gaze."

"Well," Marsali huffed, irritation evident, "we will fix that."

"Nay, please. If he must wed another for the good of the clan, how can I stand in the way? But in that case, I must leave MacNabb."

Marsali planted her fists on her hips. "Ye must stand up for yerself. Confront him. If he repudiates ye, then ye will ken ye must leave."

Fenella shook her head. "I tried once. He wouldna speak to me. I dinna ken if I can try again. I couldna bear to hear the words from his lips."

"If ye are truly to leave him behind, ye must. It will do ye nay good to go to Murray and continue to pine for Keenan."

Marsali was right. Fenella knew it. But she didn't know if she had the strength to do what she suggested, or if her heart would survive another attempt.

"Ye must try again. What if he realizes how poorly he's treated ye, and is sorry for it? What if he still wants to wed with ye," Marsali insisted, "but has simply been swept up in the day-to-day tasks he must now take responsibility for?"

What if he still loved her? Fenella shook her head. He'd closed his eyes rather than look at her. Since their aborted wedding, she'd become invisible to him—literally. "Ye didna see him in the hall when I tried to make him speak to me. To see me. 'Tis over, Marsali."

"I will write a letter to my da," Marsali promised, "that ye can take with ye, should the need arise. Gavan can escort ye. Murray will welcome ye." She held up a hand. "But if ye wish to stay—for yer sake or for wee Máirín's, talk to Keenan first, so if ye must, ye can leave with a clear mind and heart. Ye must give him a chance. Give both of ye a chance."

She was right. Fenella had to fight if she wanted the future she'd almost had in her grasp. She would find the strength to get through to him. Or leave him and MacN-abb. "Very well."

Fenella's resolve lasted long enough to get her to the laird's solar. But it was empty. Not knowing where Keenan might be, she went next to the nursery. Both Kyla and the infant were gone as well. Perhaps the nurse had taken

Máirín to Keenan's chamber for a visit with her father. The thought warmed Fenella but hurt as well. Why would he not have her bring his daughter to him? It was one more indication that he was through with her.

Fenella hoped Marsali finished the letter to her father soon.

Hours later, she heard raised voices coming from the laird's solar as Keenan met with his advisors. Rather than worrying her, knowing his time was taken up by the responsibilities of his new position gave her a little comfort, but not enough to drive the thought of going to Murray from her mind.

What did worry her was that no one she asked had seen Kyla or Keenan's daughter. Fenella searched the keep, then headed outside. Where could the nurse have taken her?

When Fenella failed to find them in the usual places the nurse might go, Fenella's concern grew. She headed out of the keep's gates into the glen. Kyla knew Fenella took the bairn outside at times. Surely the nurse would not have gone far from the keep with the laird's daughter. But Fenella met no one.

She returned to the keep and entered the great hall just as the council was leaving the laird's solar. She didn't want to face Keenan, but he needed to know his daughter was missing.

He was standing behind his desk when she entered, and his brothers were standing with him. What had happened during the council meeting that they remained behind?

Gavan noticed her first. "Fenella. Is something amiss?"

Keenan frowned at her, nearly stealing her resolve and making it harder for her to speak.

"I canna find Máirín or her nurse. I've been all through the keep and along the edge of the woods." The words hurt her, but she knew they would hurt Keenan more.

"Missing? How can a nurse and a bairn go missing?" Keenan's brother Gregor gave her a suspicious frown. "Is this some plan of yers to keep the bairn for yerself?"

The blood drained from Fenella's face as Keenan's expression turned fierce. "How could ye ask such a thing?" she stammered. "I just spent the morning looking for her." And she'd told Marsali she didn't know how she could leave the wee lass. What would Keenan think if he heard that?

"Dinna fash," Gavan told her. "We'll have some men retrace yer steps. They have to be somewhere in the keep." His assurance soothed her, but Keenan's accusatory silence hurt.

Instead of responding, she nodded to Gavan, and left the men to set up the search. Keenan's silence stung. He hadn't defended her. He hadn't spoken out to accuse her of anything either, but that was cold comfort. She had to forget him and concentrate. Where would Kyla have taken Máirín? It didn't make sense for them to disappear. What if one of them was ill or hurt?

With that thought, she went back to the healer, but she still hadn't seen them. Frustrated, Fenella returned to her chamber. Where could they be?

Hours later, Gavan fetched her. "The laird has summoned ye," he told her.

The laird, not Keenan. That didn't sound good at all. She nodded and went with him to the laird's solar.

Keenan didn't waste any time. "The nurse is back in the keep. She says she was in the village and didna have Máirín with her. She accuses ye." His jaw flexed. "I once told ye that ye loved Máirín more than me. Is that why ye took her? To keep her, and to hurt me?"

"What?" Shock stole the strength from Fenella's legs and she sank into a chair. "Nay! I'm the one who told ye she was missing."

"According to the nurse, ye decided when we were to wed that ye no longer wanted to raise another woman's child. That yers would be the MacNabb heirs."

"Ye are daft. What difference would our wedding have made except to make her truly mine? Besides, yer first son will be the MacNabb heir, nay Máirín."

"Is it daft?" Keenan's stare was hard and penetrating. "Where have ye taken her, Fenella?"

Tears pricked the back of her eyes, but she refused to shed them. She glanced at Gavan, hoping to find some sympathy there, but he'd schooled his expression into one of granite. Had Marsali already told him she was thinking of fleeing to Murray?

Gregor scowled at her. "Or where have ye buried her?"

Keenan blanched.

Fenella couldn't hold back a cry at that accusation. The image of Máirín's wee body wrapped in a shroud and laid in a shallow grave undid her. Tears flowed and would not stop, no matter how she wiped them away. "Nay, please dinna let her be dead."

Gavan's hand gripped her shoulder at that.

Keenan remained behind his desk, his gaze sick and stormy.

Gregor had moved by the door, as if to prevent her from running through it. He, too, wore a mask of stone.

"Gregor, ye go too far," Gavan objected. "Fenella raised the alarm. Why would she do that if she'd harmed Keenan's daughter?"

Finally! Gavan's forceful tone told her he believed her. She was thankful that someone did.

Keenan broke the tense silence. "I dinna want to think the woman I almost married capable of such an act, but I have been told ye are thinking of leaving MacNabb for Murray. With my daughter?"

His attempt to sound reasonable after Gregor's awful attack told her he knew. Likely Marsali told Gavan, and perhaps he had tried to convince Keenan he was about to lose Fenella forever. And that was the reason Keenan now believed she could steal his daughter. No wonder he blamed her.

"Ye said Kyla claimed she was in the village, aye? But ye didna find her when ye went there?"

Keenan frowned and glanced over her shoulder at Gregor. From the sudden increase in tension in the room, she knew he hadn't tried very hard.

"I went to her mother's croft," Gregor said. "She denied seeing Kyla since the day before. The men with me spoke to two women on the way. The village men are out in the fields."

As if the village men would pay attention to Kyla's comings and goings. If she'd gone there openly, the women should have seen her, even spoken to her. But if she'd snuck out of the keep before sunrise...

Hope filled Fenella's chest, expanding it and giving her room to breathe, and to think. Something she'd overheard the wet nurse say a few days ago worried at the back of her mind. The memory wouldn't come clear. "Someone is visiting," she muttered, and suddenly she knew. "Someone who used to live here, who married away. Who is childless," she said, raising the volume of her voice with each fragment of a memory she recalled. "I think Kyla took yer daughter to her friend. If we're lucky, she hasna yet left the village to return to her home."

"Where is the friend staying?"

Gavan asked the question, not Keenan, but a glimmer of hope flickered in Keenan's gaze. She prayed she was right. He would not be able to bear having the hope she offered for his daughter dashed.

"I dinna ken," Fenella admitted. "Ye must ask Kyla."

"Gavan, find the nurse. I'll organize the search of the village this time," Keenan said with a frown at Gregor, surprising Fenella at his sudden, commanding tone. He, too, saw that Gregor believed she was guilty and hadn't done a thorough search.

Gavan signaled to Gregor and they both left without another word.

Fenella missed the heat of Gavan's hand on her shoulder. Even more, she missed Keenan's touch. His trust. His love for her. Had she been fooled all along by a man who simply chose her as the most likely mother for his bairns?

"Fenella, if this is true, ye have my deepest apologies. But if ye have lied, it will not go well for ye. Stay here. Dinna try to move from this solar until I return. Someone will be outside the door."

Stymied, sick to her stomach, and weak with fear at being made a prisoner, Fenella could do nothing but obey.

Less than two hours later, the men returned from the village, Keenan entering the solar with Máirín in his arms, asleep on his shoulder, his relief evident in the way he clasped her to his chest. Gavan entered behind him with the nurse's arm firmly in his grip, lips pursed as though fighting to keep from berating her. Another guard brought a strange woman in behind them, and scowling Gregor brought up the rear. Both women wore fearful expressions, and tear tracks marred their faces.

Fenella leaned forward, intending to stand and take

Keenan's daughter from his arms so he could deal with the women, but Gavan caught her eye and shook his head, so she sat back.

"Who conceived of this plot against my daughter and me?" Keenan demanded once all were present.

"She did," the wet nurse spat, glaring at Fenella.

Fury replaced the fear and shock that had kept Fenella passive since Keenan left her in the solar. "I did nay such thing!"

"Did ye or nay? Ye conveniently revealed the plan and implicated the others when ye were accused," Gregor groused.

How could she defend herself against that? She couldn't. "I didna." Even to her ears, her refusal sounded weak.

Gavan spoke up, his gaze on the bairn in Keenan's arms. "Fenella saved yer daughter. She doesna deserve this."

The second woman broke her silence. "She," she said, indicating Kyla, "told me there was a motherless child in the keep. I lost mine a few months ago and wished for another. But she didna tell me she was going to take the laird's daughter! Ye are such a fool," she added with venom, turning to glare at the wet nurse.

Fenella dropped her head into her hands as relief made her too weak to hold it up.

"And this woman, " Gavan said, indicating Fenella, "had naught to do with this plot?"

Fenella lifted her head to stare at the stranger.

"Nay, I dinna ken her."

Keenan's gaze rested for a moment on Fenella, giving her the sense he was making sure she was alright. She tried to hold his gaze, to give herself a moment of feeling he still cared for her.

But his gaze shifted to the wet nurse and hardened. "What have ye to say for yerself?"

Kyla shook her head and refused to speak.

"Verra well." Keenan clenched his free hand, and frowned at the wet nurse. "I could have ye hanged—" He paused when both women gasped. "But my daughter is unharmed. Therefore, I will show ye more mercy than ye showed me. I banish ye."

"My son!" Kyla cried.

"He may go with ye. Gather yer belongings and leave with yer friend. Immediately. Perhaps she'll take ye in. I dinna care. Neither of ye are welcome at MacNabb. Ye will do nay more harm here." He shifted his gaze to Gavan. "Remove them."

Once all the others were gone, Keenan came from behind the desk and took a seat next to Fenella, his daughter still sleeping on his shoulder. "Lass, I am so dreadfully sorry."

She had not seen him look so defeated since his wife's funeral. For a moment, she wanted to react with sympathy, but found she couldn't summon any. "As ye should be," she told him, a touch of her confidence returning.

"Aye, as I should be. I was crazed with fear for Máirín."

"And so ye didna care whom ye harmed in the meantime. And since ye became laird? Since our wedding day fell to ruin? Ye havena cared about me at all."

"I have, lass. But I couldna get away from my duties to tell ye. To show ye."

He reached for her, but she leaned back, denying his touch. "It would have taken only a moment. A glance. A smile. Yet ye gave me nothing, even when I confronted ye. And to accuse me of stealing, or worse, killing yer daughter? How do ye expect me to get over that?"

He straightened, anger sparking for a moment under his creased brow. "That was Gregor's idea, nay mine." Then he dropped his shoulders, and his expression softened toward her. "I couldna believe such a thing of ye, but I could believe ye loved her enough to want her with ye, especially when I treated ye so badly ye thought ye must leave the clan."

"The nurse told me ye had received an offer of a dowry large enough to make MacNabb wealthy. I couldna stay and see ye married to another."

Keenan sighed and dropped his gaze to his hands. "I'm so sorry."

"So 'twas true? If only ye had talked to me, none of this might have happened."

The silence stretched between them, setting her teeth on edge.

"Fenella, I dinna ken who I am anymore. I didna

expect to take on this role for years. Certainly not in the midst of wedding the woman I love. The woman I owe so much to."

"What love? Ye just admitted ye were only going to marry me to settle a debt to me. If ye loved me, ye would have never treated me the way ye have since…"

"Nay, 'tisna what I meant." He shifted his daughter on his shoulder. She squirmed, then fell asleep again.

"I'll admit I was seduced by the idea of the offers of marriage and the choice of dowries MacNabb would have gained. But every time I thought of ye, I couldna choose another. I froze. Responsibilities my da seemed to handle easily overwhelmed me. Even my mother added to the burdens, nagging me to fix things da never took care of."

He looked away and Fenella thought he had finished with his excuses, none of which she could accept.

But then he continued. "Every time I tried to come to ye, someone intercepted me. Waylaid me and kept me from ye. Or I envisioned how hard it would be to have this conversation with ye." He fixed his gaze on hers. "'Tis why I couldna speak to ye in the hall that eve. I couldna admit that I hid behind my responsibilities rather than confess to ye that ye might be one more burden than I could handle. I had no time to myself to think."

Fenella looked away. "Ye thought of me as a burden rather than the one person ye most needed by yer side to *ease* yer burdens," she said softly, as though to herself, as if he was not with her while she digested his rejection. "If only ye had done as yer mother requested of the priest even as she stood over her husband's body. As yer wife, I could have helped ye." Fenella clenched her fists in her lap. "Is this any easier now that ye accused me of far worse than expecting to be yer wife?"

"Ye ken it isna. I do love ye."

He reached for her again, but she shook her head, stopping him.

His free hand dropped to the arm holding his daughter to his shoulder, as though he crossed his arms protectively over his chest. Because of the bairn he held? Or because he was trying to show her remorse?

"Dinna lie to me," she demanded, raising a palm to him. "On top of everything else, dinna do that. All I ever wanted was to help her, and to help ye," Fenella told him, nodding to the sleeping bairn. "I love ye. I was about to marry ye. Yet when ye needed me most, ye shut me out. Ye wouldna look at me. So dinna say ye love me. Ye dinna love me at all."

His eyes squeezed shut, and suddenly she was back in that dark hallway, when he closed his eyes and walked away, leaving her bereft.

"I do love ye." Then he met her gaze. "I dinna ken how to make ye see—and I'm more sorry than I can ever say— that I can ever make up to ye—that I forgot it for a while."

"Forgot? Forgot!" Outrage pushed Fenella to her feet and loomed over him. "What am I to do if ye ever forget again? What am I to do after this day? I canna compete with the offers ye were given. I am nay worth ye giving up a dowry that will enrich MacNabb." She stepped back before she woke Máirín. "And I dinna ken how my heart can heal after what ye said to me today," she added, more softly. "How ye have treated me since our wed—" She choked, unable to say the word.

He pressed his lips together, but his eyes beseeched her. "I pray ye will forget today and that day. And all the days in between. I want to go back to the way we were, standing on the kirk steps, before da..."

"Changed everything, I ken it." She took another step away from him. "I dinna ken how."

Suddenly his demeanor changed. He straightened and sat forward. "I do. Fenella, love, if ye ever trusted me, trust me now." Máirín shifted on his shoulder and he patted her back to settle her, then turned his attention back to Fenella.

"Give me time to show ye how much I love ye. Take all the time ye need to learn to trust me again. A month, a year, I will wait for ye. Talk to my family. They can tell ye things I couldna before now, things ye dinna want to hear from me, but perhaps ye will accept from them. Please... will ye give me that chance?"

"Are ye daft?" Fear filled Fenella, but resolve replaced it when he slumped and his gaze dropped to the floor at his feet. Her reaction grieved him, that was clear. But what did he expect? How could he think she would trust him again after today?

Yet, she wanted to. Looking at him holding his daughter, the wee lass she also loved, even if it was the most foolish thing she ever did, her wounded heart was willing to try.

She thought back over the time they'd had together since Máirín was born. How she'd helped him move through his grief, how she'd rejoiced to see him smile—even laugh—after months of acting as though he had died with his wife. How he'd warmed to her. Courted her. Appreciated everything she'd done for Máirín—and for him. That man, that Keenan was still in him somewhere. She hoped the time since he became laird was an aberration, or a reflection of the grieving he'd done for his wife that he'd now had to do again for his father, all while picking up his burdens.

"I need ye to steady me," he said, softly, as though hearing her thoughts. As though he wasn't sure he wanted anyone—even her—to hear him admit to weakness. "Without ye these past weeks, I've flailed. I've stumbled. I havena been the laird I need to be."

"That much is clear." It was an uncharitable thing to say, but her injuries were still fresh, and she needed him to know how deeply his actions had hurt her.

"I dinna ken if I can do this without ye, Fenella. I dinna want to find out. I do love ye. I want ye to remember that. To think back to before the day we were to wed. My feelings for ye never wavered, despite how I acted."

Máirín chose that moment to start to fuss. Keenan

tried to soothe her, but in moments, she was wailing in his ear.

"Give her to me," Fenella told him, reaching for the bairn. "Send for yer family. Yer mother, brothers, and Marsali. I want them to hear what ye have said to me. If they believe ye, I will ken that I can as well."

"I'll do anything ye wish," he told her on a deep breath.

She cuddled his daughter, who stopped crying and watched her with wide, guileless eyes. Fenella's chest swelled with love for this wee lass. How could she abandon her? But how could she trust her father?

When the rest of the family arrived, Keenan announced, "Fenella requested ye all hear what I have said to her, so that ye may judge whether she can trust me or nay." He stood tall and confessed it all, every fear, every misstep, every slight he'd inflicted on her, including many things Fenella had not been aware of. Gasps greeted his words. But as he finished, so did smiles.

Fenella regretted putting him through this, but the expressions on his family's faces told her the truth Keenan wanted her to see and hear. He was sincere. His mother summed it up. "Ach, Keenan, ye nearly threw away the woman ye love, and the mother to yer daughter. I'm glad to see ye coming to yer senses. If ye didna, Gregor would have to marry her, for I will have her for a daughter, nay matter if 'tis despite ye."

That got a laugh from everyone except Fenella and Gregor, whose face turned ashen. As much as Fenella appreciated his mother's sentiment, Gregor had been her harshest accuser. She couldn't look at him, much less think to marry him. His dismay at his mother's jest served him right, but she dreaded that comment being repeated and the jests it would inspire about her running out of brothers to *almost* wed.

"Dinna fash, brother," Keenan told him. "She's mine, and I willna give her up. If she'll have me."

When he stopped talking and turned to her, she took a breath and went to his side. She believed him.

He put an arm around her waist, and careful not to dislodge her hold on his daughter, leaned in and whispered, "So ye will take the time I offered ye?"

She shook her head. "Nay." At his crestfallen look, she added, "I dinna need it."

He straightened, hope in his eyes. "Then marry me now. I will call the priest to marry us here. With any witnesses ye care to name. Trust me, Fenella. Marry me, love me, and be the mother to our bairns."

Warmth filled her, and relief eased the ache in her chest. "I will."

Keenan kissed her then, and her heart soared. His kiss was sweet, gentle, yet full of promise. It was the kiss of the Keenan she had fallen in love with and had hoped was still inside him. Despite all the hurt, the fear, and the anger that had fallen between them, she believed they loved each other enough to make a good life together, no matter what else came their way.

She wouldn't even object to Gregor remaining for the ceremony. She suspected that despite having escorted the wet nurse away from MacNabb, he would need to see his brother wed her to fully believe in her innocence.

Keenan called for a lad to fetch the priest, then turned to his family. "We await only the priest to be wed. To right the wrongs I have done to Fenella and to prove my love for her. To regain the trust she freely gave that I abused."

"Ye certainly did," Gavan muttered, making Keenan wince.

The priest entered then and Keenan explained again why they were gathered. Gavan stood by his brother, pulled a length of the MacNabb plaid from his shoulder and handed it to the priest for the hand fasting.

"We want more than that first step," Keenan demanded. "We will be wed, but here rather than at the kirk."

"I understand," the priest said, cognizant of the pain of the old laird's recent death there. His agreement gave Fenella a much needed sense of anticipation. Her heart fluttered in her chest, butterfly wings tickling the insides of her ribs and belly.

Before the priest could start, Marsali pulled a rolled parchment from her sleeve, and with her gaze on Fenella, unrolled it, tore it in half, and tossed it on the fire.

"What are ye doing?" Keenan demanded, his sharp tone making Máirín rouse and cry out. Fenella soothed her and she dropped off to sleep again.

"Fenella can tell ye later," Marsali said softly, her gaze on the bairn. "Yer mother is right. Ye being boneheaded nearly cost ye everything worth having in this life. 'Tis glad I am to see ye have come to yer senses."

Fenella smiled at her friend, grateful that she'd been willing to help, and glad her help was no longer needed.

Keenan gave Fenella a quizzical look which she waved off. If he thought for a moment, he'd realize Marsali had destroyed a letter to her father. If not, she'd tell him later.

At Keenan's urging, Fenella handed Máirín to Marsali. Once Fenella was unburdened, he nodded to the priest to begin.

The priest performed the hand fasting according to the old ways, then an abbreviated ceremony of marriage. As he finished, a lad arrived with the register of marriage from the kirk for them to sign.

The priest handed Keenan the quill, and Fenella held her breath as he bent to sign his name. The sense of rightness that had filled her all those days ago on the kirk's steps came back into her. It was over. Despite what had come between them since that day, nothing ever would again.

Keenan took Fenella in his arms and kissed her soundly.

"'Tis done, wife," he told her.

"Lady MacNabb," his mother added and handed her the ring of chatelaine's keys. "Ye have chosen well, laird."

"About time," Marsali muttered, eliciting a laugh from everyone, including wee Máirín.

Their approval gave Fenella the confidence to face Keenan's family with a smile. She belonged with them now, as she had long wished to do. MacNabb would thrive, and so would their marriage and the family they would make together.

HIGHLAND FURY'S LEGACY

Jamie Lathan has been a favorite character of mine and my fans since I first introduced him in HIGHLAND HEALER. *He appeared in* HIGHLAND SEER *and finally got his own love story in* HIGHLAND TROTH.

I always felt the friendship between young Jamie and his cousin Toran Lathan wanted more light shed on it, especially during the time when Caitrin, the Fletcher heir, fostered at Lathan. Her presence annoyed Toran, but she fascinated Jamie and made him hope for a future with her.

Yet, along with Jamie, she was party to a horrifying event that changed the course of their young lives. To protect her, the Lathan laird, Toran's father, sent her home. The tragedy and double loss that resulted from it so deeply traumatized Jamie, they led to the final violent confrontation in HIGHLAND TROTH.

"Damn it, Jamie, she's following us again." Toran's complaint, hissed between his teeth, matched the glare in his eyes as he and Jamie raced down the path from the Aerie to the glen below the tor.

"And 'tis my fault?" Jamie retorted after a glance over his shoulder. Fourteen-year-old Caitrin was hard to miss, her long auburn hair flying, and coltish legs pumping to catch the two lads. She danced between two horses bound for the Aerie's gates, twisting aside without missing a step to let them pass, and kept coming.

"Ye were supposed to make certain yer sister kept her busy at her stitching, ye ken?"

"I thought ye said yer sister would do that." He thought Toran had. But he'd also told his older sister Netta to make sure Caitrin didn't follow Toran or him when they left the keep, and she'd agreed—for a price. Jamie smirked to himself. He wouldn't be helping her by collecting the herbs she wanted after all. He didn't know what price Toran's sister—or even which sister—had exacted, but it seemed they couldn't count on any of their sisters.

He and Toran reached the glen and raced across it to the woods, where they changed direction. "'Tis a bad idea, Toran," Jamie warned. Toran hoped to lose their follower in the thick undergrowth and trees. But Caitrin was nearly as fast as they were. Or faster. They heard twigs snapping and the occasional girlish oath as the low evergreen branches slapped at her or she tripped over raised roots, but she never gave up, though she was still behind them.

Toran had no patience when it came to Caitrin Fletcher. But something about her had attracted Jamie from the moment he first saw her. He liked her laugh and how determined she was to accomplish anything the lads did—and to beat them if she could. Those seemed to him to be excellent qualities in a laird's only heir, male or female. And Caitrin was the Fletcher heir, which was why, no matter that it was unusual to foster away a lass, she was now chasing him and Toran into the trees near the clan Lathan stronghold, and not doing embroidery under the watchful eye of her nurse in her chamber at Fletcher.

"She's still gaining on us," Toran complained as he took another turn, hoping to confuse their trail.

Jamie paused and looked back, but didn't see her. He

wanted to. She was pleasing to look at, with thick hair that fell to her waist in shimmering waves, bright eyes that crinkled when she smiled—and that laugh. It drew Jamie like Cook's honey cakes, sweetly rich and irresistible.

But Jamie would be laughed out of the keep if he deserted Toran to take care of an almost three-years-younger lass. Though Toran was not the eldest and heir, he was the laird's son.

Toran ducked into a tangle of undergrowth between two oaks and hunkered down against one of the trees. Jamie knew he expected Caitrin to run right past them if she was still on their trail. She'd gone quiet, so Jamie ran past Toran's location and slid behind a broad pine to listen for her. Once his breathing slowed and quieted, he heard nothing else except for birdcalls and leaves rustling in the highland wind. It seemed they'd lost her. Toran would be pleased. They could hunt coneys without Caitrin deliber-ately making noise and scaring away their prey. But Jamie's lips tightened in disappointment. Opportunities to spend time with her were rare. Even if he had to do so with Toran shooting frowns at him behind her back, Jamie would relish the chance.

The longer they waited, the less comfortable Jamie felt, his gut knotting more and more as time passed. Bird calls and wind rustling in the trees continued to be all he heard, and they were all normal forest sounds. Caitrin couldn't be anywhere near them or the birds would have gone silent as she approached. Or she would have made some noise that gave her away as she tried to sneak up on them. But he heard nothing. She must have lost their trail and gone another way. That worried him.

The hunt Toran had proposed seemed a good idea at the time. Cook always welcomed coneys for stew or to add meat to other dishes, but losing Caitrin in these woods struck Jamie as unkind—and foolish. She didn't know her way around in the trees and thick undergrowth as well as they did.

Suddenly convinced that she would get lost and not find her way back to the Aerie, he tangled his fingers in his hair, clenched his fist, and tugged, then did what he knew was right. Toran would be annoyed, but he stepped out of cover anyway. He could put up with Toran's complaints— or worse, his teasing that Jamie was sweet on the lass. He no longer cared. If Caitrin had gone straight where they made their last turn, she'd be deep in the woods and headed for rougher ground. Wolves lived in these woods, as did other predators. A lass alone would not be able to defend herself.

No longer interested in concealment, he stomped over to where Toran hid, careless of the noise he made. "Enough," Jamie told him. "She might be in trouble soon, if she is nay already. We need to find her."

"Shite, Jami—" Toran's complaint cut off mid-word.

"Nay, ye dinna," Caitrin said over him, her voice

coming from shockingly close. "Ye can try to lose me, but ye willna."

Her taunt made Toran growl and stand. "Ye canna come with us," he insisted, turning his head toward the source of the girlish voice and raising his. "We're hunting coneys. Ye always scare them away."

"Truly?" She stepped out from concealment behind a nearby tree and held up two, her fist around their long ears. "How many do ye have?"

Shock sent heat through Jamie in a wave. "How did ye have time to do that and still find us?" And how did the lass who used to spoil their hunts with her sympathy for the "wee beasties" now present them with two of her own kills?

Caitrin smirked at Toran, and Jamie wanted to applaud her backbone. "I'll never tell," she taunted.

"I dinna care if ye do or nay," Toran told her. "Take those back to Cook. We'll bring more."

Jamie could see Toran was impressed and fighting to hide it. His shoulders had tensed, though he kept his hands open and loose.

Her gaze moved from Toran to Jamie. "I'd rather stay with ye. I can help." She didn't plead. She simply made her case, impressing Jamie yet again.

Toran shook his head. "Nay, ye canna. These woods are nay place for a lass alone—"

Jamie frowned at Toran. Until she showed up and beat

him at his own game, he'd been fine leading her a merry chase all through these woods.

"I willna be alone," she argued, her gaze shifting quickly to Toran as she made her point, then back to Jamie. "I'll be with ye." She held his gaze, challenge and something else sparking from her eyes.

Jamie's pulse quickened. What was she implying? She'd always seemed to want Toran's attention, but her gaze stayed locked with his, as if Toran was not with them. Had she finally realized he was more her friend than Toran would ever be?

"Ye canna fight," Toran insisted. "Ye'll be a danger to us if we have to protect ye."

Color bloomed across her cheeks and nose. She narrowed her eyes at Toran's words, and the flush on her face told Jamie she was still in a mood to fight him. This was getting them nowhere.

"I'll go back with ye to the keep," Jamie said. The words were out before he gave them any thought. And the look Toran gave him promised trouble later. But in this, Toran was right. If they were attacked — by wolves or anything else, she'd be a liability. "Toran can carry on. While we go, we may add to yer count, and later, we'll see if he can match what ye caught."

Caitrin gave him a grateful look and nodded.

Toran huffed out a breath and aimed a glare at Jamie. "Go on with ye, then. I've work to do for both of us now that ye would rather spend time with a lass."

Jamie met Toran's glare with a shrug Toran was welcome to interpret any way he liked, then gestured for Caitrin to precede him.

Behind her back, Toran grinned. Jamie turned his, telling Toran he was not pleased with his behavior. Not that Toran would care. He'd gotten his way.

Both Jamie and Caitrin took down two more coneys on the edge of the glen. Inside the Aerie's gates, they headed for the kitchen and gave Cook the rabbits.

"Thank ye, Jamie," she told him after a nod to Caitrin.

"Dinna thank me," he told Cook. "Most of those are Caitrin's contribution."

"Well done, lass. Thank ye."

Caitrin smiled at the praise.

"Do ye ken yer herbs as well as how to catch game?"

"I do," Caitrin responded. "What do ye need?"

Cook mentioned several herbs. "They grow in the glen and along the woods, nay in the Aerie's garden. The next time ye venture out of the keep, ye might keep an eye out for them."

"I'm pleased to be of help to ye," Caitrin told her. "We can go back down now."

Jamie kept his groan to himself. What Caitrin proposed was exactly what his sister wanted him to do. But this would be with Caitrin. Alone. "Aye, we can, Cook," he said, "if ye need these things today."

"I need them every day to flavor yer food," she reminded him. "Better fresh, though I dry some to use during the winter. And many are useful in poultices and the like. Ye might ask the healer before ye go."

Well, that put a point to it. He'd not talk Caitrin out of this errand now. Not when she could contribute to Cook *and* the healer.

"Will ye truly go back with me, Jamie? Toran seemed concerned..."

Toran concerned? Well, true, but he had been more concerned with sending her back up the tor and out of his hair than he had been with her safety. "Of course I will." No one would keep him from the chance to spend time alone with her. Those opportunities were rare, indeed, in a busy keep like the Aerie. And with Toran occupied elsewhere, Jamie might have the time he needed to find out more about Caitrin, and to discern where her affections were directed—at Toran, as he'd always thought, or at him. The looks she'd given him earlier in the woods made him hope for the latter.

After Caitrin collected a basket from Cook for the herbs, they visited the healer to find out what she needed, then went back down the trail to the glen. The day had warmed from the morning chill. Bees and butterflies danced from flower to flower, making the grasses and shrubs filling the glen seem alive with sound and motion.

"'Tis bonnie, aye?" Jamie kept his gaze firmly on the hills in the distance, but what he truly meant was Caitrin. Yet he dared not tell her, not in so many words, and not yet.

Not until he knew he'd been right to think she wanted to spend time alone with him, and not with Toran.

"Aye. And look! There are the cowberries both Cook and the healer need." Caitrin moved quickly to pluck several handfuls while she set Jamie to gathering wild onions for the kitchen.

After an hour of silent toil, broken only by her exclamations when she discovered another plant needed in the keep, Jamie realized he would have to be happy to watch her hair in the light and her shape as she moved and stretched for the plant she intended to pick. She fascinated him—and he wished she felt the same about him, but from the corner of his eye, he hadn't caught her gaze straying to him. Not even once. She'd ignored him save to ask his help to dig up something she couldn't pull from the ground. He was beginning to give up hope of having enough of a conversation to understand her feelings.

Finally, they moved under the shade of the forest lining the glen. Jamie hoped Toran was nowhere nearby. Or that he had already gone back up to the keep, taking more coneys to Cook. They hadn't seen him, but he could have gotten by them easily. Jamie's attention had been divided by their quest and Caitrin's nearness. And a general watchful eye for predators, even more acute now that they had ventured under the trees.

Before long, Caitrin's basket was full enough for Jamie to insist on carrying it for her. He kept watch while she searched for more herbs. The Aerie's tor was out of sight now, behind rows of trees, which meant they were out of sight of the guards on the Aerie's walls. If trouble found them here, they would have to meet it on the strength of Jamie's dirk and *sgian dubh*. He started wishing he had a claymore on his back, then chided himself for being foolishly anxious. He and Toran had explored these woods countless times with no problems. He had no reason to expect any today.

Except that Caitrin was with him. He would protect her with his life.

"Ach, nay!" Her outcry startled Jamie out of his thoughts but sent a surge of adrenaline rushing into his blood. He spun to face her, concerned at the frown that had replaced her usually sunny expression. Blood streaked the back of her hand.

"What's amiss, lass? What happened?"

"I'm daft as a stick," she complained and bent to tear a bit of cloth from her undershift, exposing her low boot and trim woolen-stocking-clad ankle.

Jamie would have enjoyed the view save for the blood on her hand.

"I canna do it. Jamie, can ye help me?"

He set the basket aside and knelt by her foot. "Of course. Let me see." He took her hand in his and studied the wound on its back. Not a snake bite, thank the saints. A long scratch. Deep enough to bleed freely, it dripped warm blood onto his hand.

"I went after some berries as a treat for us in that patch

of brambles," Caitrin told him with a nod in its direction. "Instead of just picking the new leaves the healer wanted and leaving the berries for the animals."

"'Tis deep enough, it does need to be wrapped."

"Ye can tear a length from my shift's hem. When ye are done, we still need to pick some leaves."

He bent to tear the cloth as she directed, tempted, but for the circumstances, to touch her ankle, to run a hand up her calf to see if her legs were as strong with muscle as he thought they must be. But that would be improper in the extreme. He retrieved the cloth, muttering, "I hope this wasna yer favorite shift."

Caitrin laughed softly.

Jamie glanced up and nearly choked at the gleam in her eyes as she watched him. If he had the nerve, he'd stand and kiss her, right then and there. But instead, he grinned, took her hand and gently bound it in the cloth. "That should stop the bleeding and protect it until we get back. "The healer will tend it. Likely, ye will have a scar, but mayhap nay." If she did, would looking at it remind her of him?

"Thank ye, Jamie," she told him, inspecting his work. "Thank ye for coming with me, and thank ye for taking care of me."

He stood, and her gaze lifted to meet his. "I will always take care of ye, lass. I care about ye."

"I ken ye do."

Something in her tone gave her words extra weight, but before Jamie asked how or why, she spoke again.

"And I for ye, Jamie Lathan." She lifted her uninjured hand to his cheek. "Ye are a good friend to me. One I will treasure always."

Jamie's heart lifted at her words. "As I treasure ye, Caitrin," he said, his voice dropping soft and deep. He laid his hand over her smaller one. "More than ye ken." Should he kiss her? Would she welcome it?

Her gaze shifted to the side.

He held his breath and fought back the urge.

She laid a finger over his lips and held up her other hand.

At first he thought she had divined his intention and meant to keep his lips away from hers.

But in a moment, he understood she meant to silence him. He heard what had stolen her attention from his confession.

Voices. Male voices. Unfamiliar male voices.

Jamie nodded, took her arm, and gestured with a tilt of his head toward the glen and the safety of the Aerie. Caitrin picked up the basket with her good hand. He led her that way, moving as silently as he could, his free hand on his dirk. She matched him, step for quiet step, her expression fierce, eyes narrowed and head cocked as if listening for followers.

Good lass. Jamie was proud of her courage even as he hurried them away. The voices moved deeper into the forest and soon faded. Still, he didn't take a full breath until they were out from under the trees and back in the glen, in full view of the Aerie's guards.

"Who were they?" Caitrin whispered so softly, he barely heard her over the hum of the bees floating from flower to flower.

"I dinna ken," Jamie said and pursed his lips. "'Tis unusual to have strangers this close to the Aerie."

"Ye will tell the guards, aye?" She turned and looked up at the Aerie's walls.

"Of course. The laird will send out a patrol. Now, forget them. Let's get ye to the healer to take care of yer hand."

"First we'll take our basket to Cook," she said, determination in her tone, and passed it to him when he reached for it.

"Whatever ye wish, lass," Jamie told her. He helped her up the tor, the basket in one hand and the other on Caitrin's elbow. Though she had climbed the tor quite easily on her own earlier that day, she permitted his touch, for which Jamie was grateful. She'd been hurt while with him and he wanted to care for her. Though the trip to the glen had not gone precisely as he'd hoped, he would have other chances to make her see him as more than a friend. She would be with Lathan for another year, perhaps two, before she would return to Fletcher, so he had time to win her heart—and if everything went as he hoped, someday, her hand.

He knew the daughter of a laird must make a match

advantageous to her clan, but surely her father counted on her fostering at Lathan to result in a match with a suitable Lathan lad to rule Fletcher with her, or act as her arms master or in some other highly-placed position in their clan. A lad like him, perhaps.

Toran would have a better sense of who might be considered for a female laird's husband and in what capacity, but the last thing Jamie wanted to do was raise the idea with Toran that Jamie had hopes in that direction. He would never hear the end of it, especially if she left Lathan without him, without a betrothal or even a hand fasting with him. The idea saddened him, not because it would give Toran years' worth of teasing to torture him with, but because he would lose Caitrin. Or he might plant the idea in Toran's mind, and his friend would decide to pursue her to one day become the Fletcher laird. Jamie didn't like that idea at all.

He fought the urge to say something to her. To convince her she belonged with him, and he with her. But he couldn't. Not yet. It was too soon. He had time, and today was a good start.

They sought out the guard captain and told him of the voices in the woods, then dropped the basket of herbs, flowers and berries in the kitchen with Cook to sort through. She would ensure the healer got a share of the things she could use.

Jamie insisted on escorting Caitrin to the healer. "Ye were hurt while ye were with me. I willna leave ye alone until I see ye healed," he told her. "I meant it when I said I would always take care of ye."

"The healer will care for me, Jamie. Surely ye have something more important to do."

"Aye, she will, and I'll escort ye to her," he insisted with a smile. "Ye are the most important—helping ye is the most important thing I have to do today." He feared once again that he'd said too much, but her answering smile relieved his anxiety.

"Thank ye, Jamie. Ye are a good man."

The healer greeted them when they arrived at her herbal near the kitchen. "What have ye done to yer hand?" The make-shift bandage Jamie had wrapped around it was hard to miss.

"'Tis naught," Caitrin said. "A scratch. But Jamie insisted I come to ye."

The healer nodded. "Jamie is wise beyond his years."

Jamie fought the urge to stand taller and puff out his chest at the praise. Both women were too perceptive to let him get away with that. Besides, he was too old for that sort of thing.

"Where did ye scratch yer hand?"

"In the woods, reaching into a bramble for berries. We brought Cook a basket full of herbs, berries and flowers. Some, she said, she'd save for ye."

The healer nodded as she unwrapped Caitrin's hand. "Very well. Jamie, ye needna remain."

He understood an order when he heard one and took a

reluctant step toward the door. One did not disobey the healer, especially not in her herbal.

"Thank ye, Jamie," Caitrin told him again before he went too far.

"Of course, lass. I'll speak with ye later."

Her gaze locked with his and she gave him another smile.

He took it with him, held close to his heart.

He saw Caitrin at the evening meal, but she was with a group of lasses, her friends, and he didn't intrude. She had a new bandage on her hand, one neater and cleaner than the one he'd fashioned from a strip torn from her shift. He held that memory close to his heart as well. She had allowed a familiarity, an intimacy, that he hadn't expected, though it was needful at the time. It gave him hope that she would allow that bond between them to grow into something more.

He spent the next morning training with the other younger men of the clan, paired, as he often was, with Toran.

"So how many coneys did ye give to Cook?" Jamie asked as he swung a fist at Toran's jaw. They usually trained with weapons, but the arms master insisted they be able to fight without them as well. Many battles devolved into weaponless, hand-to-hand combat. His men would be well prepared for that eventuality.

Jamie didn't really care about the coneys, but knew

Toran would have kept count, and had probably asked Cook how many they'd supplied.

Toran ducked and danced aside and around Jamie. "I beat ye by one," he answered, aiming a blow at Jamie's kidneys.

Jamie spun and took the hit on his arm, then lashed out and caught Toran on the chin, snapping his head back even though Jamie pulled the punch—a little. "Did ye, now?"

"Enough!" The arms master called out as the bell rang for the midday meal. "Get cleaned up and get inside."

Toran rubbed his chin and gave Jamie a grin. "Good shot. Did ye enjoy yer time with Caitrin?"

His smirk told Jamie he knew what Jamie had been up to in offering to escort her. "I did," Jamie answered succinctly, grabbing a length of sheeting to dry off with. "Until we heard strangers' voices in the woods. We headed back to the keep."

"Strangers?" Toran scrubbed sweat from his face and neck, eyeing Jamie.

"Men. Several. We didn't stick around to find out how many. We went one way, and from the sound of it, they were headed away from the glen, so we didn't see them."

Toran frowned. "Ye told—"

"The guard captain, aye, of course."

"Damn. That could have gone very badly."

"It didna. Let's leave it at that, aye?"

Late that afternoon, the laird called Jamie to his solar.

"I dinna want ye to *fash* overmuch," he began, "but yer sister is missing."

Jamie felt an icicle plunge into his chest. The voices in the woods filled his mind and he sank into the chair opposite the laird's desk.

"How long?"

"Since early this morning. The healer sent her to search for something she needed. She says Netta should have been back hours ago."

"Caitrin and I just brought a basket full of..." Damn, the bramble leaves. Is that what she'd gone for? The leaves they were meant to gather yesterday? Jamie's belly roiled with guilt and bile rose in his throat.

He stood, unable to sit any longer. If he didn't get out of here soon, he'd be sick in the laird's solar. "Who's looking for her? I need to help find her."

"Ye need to stay here, lad. I have men searching for her. I dinna want them to have to search for ye, too."

"There were men in the woods yesterday. Voices I didna recognize."

"Aye, the guard captain told me what ye reported to him. We will find her."

Jamie's belly gave another lurch and he felt cold sweat break out on his forehead. "Ye willna if those men took her."

"We dinna ken that, lad. She may have fallen and gotten hurt, and is waiting, kenning we'll look for her. Our men will find her and bring her to the healer. She will be well."

Jamie hoped the laird was right. But some sense he couldn't name told him her disappearance was connected to the men he and Caitrin heard the day before. He was glad he'd gone with her and had gotten her away before anyone found her. They could both be thankful for that. Now, if only his sister was as lucky and the Lathan warriors found her. Night would fall soon, and predators would roam the woods in the darkness.

Without another word, he left the solar and ran for the gate, the movement and anticipation of doing something, anything, to find his sister, helping to settle his nerves. Despite the laird's assurances, he would search for Netta. But when he reached the bailey, the gates were closed.

"No one in or out," the guard told him. "Nay 'til the searchers return."

"I go to join them," Jamie insisted. "Open the gates."

"The laird specifically forbid us to allow ye to leave," the man told him.

Jamie froze where he stood, certainty washing through him that the Lathan feared the worst and was keeping Jamie from being the one to find his sister's body. It was one thing to be lied to and coddled as though he couldn't be trusted in the woods. It was another to be locked in like a child, unable to help his sister in her time of need. His stomach twisted again and its contents threatened to erupt, but he held it down, anger tightening his muscles and locking his jaw. He spun on his heel and climbed the steps to the wall walk.

The view of the glen and the edge of the woods was unchanged. Late afternoon sunshine filled the glen and lit the tops of the trees. No one was visible. Not the searchers and not his sister. Tension made his hands shake as he lifted them to grip the bulwark he peered over. The men must have gone deeper into the woods. Perhaps even where he and Caitrin had heard the voices. If she hadn't heard them before they got too close, if he hadn't been with her, she could be missing, too. The thought of both Caitrin and his sister missing—gone—brought tears to his eyes that he'd held inside since the laird delivered the news about Netta. She'd been missing for hours, and the daylight was waning. He pounded his fists on the wall, hating the feeling of helplessness that hollowed his chest and churned his belly. He should be out there, too, searching. Instead, Jamie stood vigil until the sun set, then went down the stairs into the great hall. Toran met him there.

"I heard. I'm sorry, Jamie. They'll find her."

Jamie shook his head, unable to speak. He took a breath. "The sun just set. What are her chances in the dark?"

Toran's expression was grim, his mouth set, and his brow furrowed. They both knew the risks. "If she has yer luck, she'll be fine."

Jamie's eyes burned and he turned away, headed up the stairs to his chamber, leaving Toran and his platitudes behind. Netta was smart and if she could, she would take care of herself until help arrived. If she could.

Vision dimmed by tears, Jamie didn't see the person he bumped into in the upper hall.

"Jamie! What's amiss?"

Caitrin's voice was a balm to his tortured soul, as was her touch on his arm, gentle yet firm enough to stop him in his tracks. She was here, safe, and with him. And he needed her more than she knew. "Netta is missing in the woods," he choked out. "All day."

"Ach, nay," Caitrin said and gripped both his shoulders. "Those voices we heard…"

"Aye, 'tis what *fashes* me." He wiped his face, trying to dry the tears on his cheeks.

Before he knew it, her arms were around him, and she urged his head onto her shoulder. "I'm sorry, Jamie. I ken how hard it is to wait for news."

"The laird sent searchers," he said against her neck. Her scent filled his nose, soothing him enough to raise his head. "But he willna allow me to join them."

"They will find her." A noise on the stair startled them. "Come, let's go in yer chamber. Ye dinna need others—"

"Nay, I dinna. I need ye."

"Then let me care for ye as ye have cared for me."

Caitrin sat with him while he paced, and talked to him. He remembered none of what she said, only the soothing sound of her voice and the fact of her presence, trying to help him through his fears. Finally, exhausted, he sat on his bed. She pushed him flat, covered him with a blanket and stayed in the chair by his bed until he fell asleep.

Late the next day, the searchers returned with his sister's body wrapped in several plaids and tied over the back of a horse. No one would let Jamie see her, but he heard enough to sicken him. She'd been attacked and abused in all the ways evil men can abuse a woman alone. Her bloodied body bore the marks. Proof, he was told by someone who overheard the men who'd found her talking later that evening, of what was done to her before she died.

Jamie spent the time until they buried her in a rage, but the feverish intensity of it left his body as they lowered hers into the ground, still wrapped and hidden from his sight. He hadn't even been allowed to see her face. In place of the rage, cold fury sank into his bones, chilling him. He knew in that moment that he dared never give in to it, or he would not be responsible for his actions. For the rest of his life, he would be a danger to all around him. He would gladly have died in his sister's place. Instead, he would have to live with the knowledge of what happened to her. Of his guilt that he and Caitrin had failed to bring back the leaves the healer sent Netta for. And that his warning to the guard captain had no effect. He would always blame himself. He knew his sister went often to the glen for Cook. He should have told her about the voices, too, but he was too captivated by his outing with Caitrin and the closeness they'd shared.

Toran found him on the practice field, firing arrow after arrow into the targets set up against the outer wall.

"Jamie, stop," he commanded.

"I canna," Jamie told him as he drew and released again. "I have to get rid of the beast within me."

Toran took his arm. "There's nay such thing," Toran told him. "'Tis only yer grief, and it will pass in time."

"Will it?" Jamie dropped the bow and faced his friend. "I dinna think so. I want to kill something. Kill the men who did this. I fear I always will."

"My father has forbidden the lasses to leave the keep. And he's sending Caitrin back to Fletcher. He fears he canna protect her here."

Jamie would have expected such news to be a body blow, but he felt nothing. Still, he didn't want her to go. "So soon?"

"Tomorrow morning."

"He canna do that. She'll be in greater danger on the way." Jamie felt the beast within him raise its head.

"She's going with twenty of our best warriors. She'll be safe."

"She would be safer here. Netta should have been safe here." He half expected Toran to clasp him on the shoulder, but his friend had better sense.

"I ken it. I'm sorry."

Jamie walked away, leaving Toran to collect the bow and arrows. "Sorry doesna bring her back," he muttered. Or keep Caitrin with me, he told himself.

The next morning, as promised, twenty men mounted up with Caitrin in their midst. When she saw Jamie approaching, her eyes widened. Did she really think he would let her leave without a word? She reached out a hand from her seat on one of the Lathan's most reliable horses and the sight of the fresh bandage wrapping it nearly stopped his heart. Had it been so few days since everything changed?

"Who told ye?" Her frown said she already knew.

"Toran." He glanced aside to where the laird and Toran stood speaking to the head of Caitrin's guards at the front of the double line of horses. The wider spread of the horses around her made it look like a snake that had eaten a mouse.

"Toran." She sniffed. "He told me I'm too young to ken what's best for me and to do what I'm told."

"He isn't always right, but in this, he might be."

Caitrin's mouth dropped open and her brows lowered.

He knew his words hit her like a betrayal, but what else could he say? Neither of them could stop this.

"Ye must be safe," he insisted, putting his hand over hers where they clenched her reins. "I couldna bear to see ye hurt."

"I dinna wish to leave," she told him.

If only she'd said she didn't wish to leave *him*. But she hadn't.

"I dinna wish for ye to leave, either, Caitrin, ye ken that. But perhaps 'tis for the best." He let go of her and took a short step away, fully aware of how close the guard's horse stood behind him.

If Caitrin knew the cold hatred that lived within him now, she'd kick her horse into motion and flee from him as fast as her horse could run. He was not the same lad he'd been, wrapping her injured hand and leading her away from danger in the woods. Now he was a man with a monster inside of him, a beast that wanted to throw back its head and howl its pain and fury to the skies. He'd never get over having to abandon picking the bramble leaves that, had they collected them, would have meant his sister still lived. He didn't blame Caitrin. He swore vengeance on the men who'd killed his sister.

Caitrin's hand found his cheek, much as she'd done in the woods, and Jamie's heart stuttered again, filling his chest with agony as he recalled the night she'd put her arms around him to comfort him, and stayed in the chair next to his bed until he fell into an exhausted sleep. He would never hurt her. Would he? Not knowing scared him to his bones.

"Let's go!" The guard captain shouted as the laird and Toran stepped away from him.

"Ye canna lie to me. Ye dinna believe sending me away is for the best—for me or for ye." Caitrin's lips twisted as if she attempted a smile and failed. "Thank ye for yer care of me," she said, softly and simply, then she released him and followed her guard out the Aerie's gates and down the tor, away from him.

Face burning from her touch, Jamie stood as the guards' horses passed him on either side and watched her go. Whatever remained of the lad in him feared he'd never see her again, and worse that she'd never want to see him again. They would both be reminders for each other of his sister's loss, and the terrible way she'd died.

Perhaps the distance between them was for the best. If he ever hoped to be with Caitrin and keep her safe, he needed time to get control of himself. He would not trouble her unless she reached out to him first. If she did not, he would know the truth—she had never been his, and his dream of a future with her had been just that, a dream.

A SEASON FOR LONGING

HIGHLAND TROTH (Highland Talents Series Book 6) explores the history and romance of Jamie Lathan and Caitrin Fletcher. A few years after that book ends, the Yuletide season is upon them. It should be a happy time, but Caitrin's father, the Fletcher laird, is getting older and forgetful. And his wife, gone home to MacGregor for a visit, is late returning. And she's not the only one who goes missing.

Enjoy this new story of Christmas miracles.

Wind whistled down the chimney as Laird Fletcher struggled to pull a heavy tartan plaid over his withered leg. Most of the clan remained in the great hall after the evening meal. Deep mid-winter darkness had fallen hours ago and it seemed to Caitrin that no one was eager to leave the bright warmth of the hall or each others' company.

"Let me get that for ye." Caitrin set aside her needlework and stood. She hated to see her father fret, and in his condition, he must be kept warm.

"Wheesht, Daughter. I'm no' helpless." He righted the cover and settled back into his chair set before the merrily dancing flames in the Fletcher great hall's hearth. "'Tis only that I feel in my bones a storm's coming. Have we any word yet?"

His wife Lady Madeleine's absence had troubled Fletcher all the weeks she'd been gone. As the highland winter deepened into unrelenting cold and dark, he seemed to shrink in on himself. Caitrin and her husband, Jamie Lathan, did what they could to keep him active and involved in running the clan, but it was clear the Fletcher's days in charge were numbered, and the burdens she and Jamie bore for him would soon be theirs in truth.

Caitrin frowned at her father, whose gaze had returned to the fire in the hearth. She turned to Jamie and shrugged. Da's moods shifted like those of a bairn. Jamie had a way with him, and she wanted him to keep her da calm.

Jamie nodded and got up from his seat to stir the fire. "Ye need no' *fash*. Lady Madeleine will be home before ye ken it."

"If the storm brings snow, she might be forced to turn back."

"A little snow willna stop her returning to ye," Caitrin told him.

Jamie set aside the wrought iron poker and turned to face his father-in-law. "And just think, soon the days will lengthen into spring."

"Ach, there's the innocence of youth," Fletcher groused. "We've the darkest part of winter before us." His eyes drifted closed. "Ah, but I recall the Beltane fires of my own youth," he added with a lift to the corners of his mouth. "Such revelry after a long, bleak winter. 'Tis a shame I didna ken Madeleine in those days."

Caitrin's heart lifted. He'd thought of something that pleased him. "Ye wouldha' made quite a pair." And perhaps all the misery at MacGregor that had happened in the years since would not have occurred. She forced herself to set that thought aside. "And we've a celebration ye can enjoy much sooner than Beltane," she reminded him.

"But what if she arrives too late?"

"Lady Madeleine willna disappoint ye, Da." Caitrin had to believe that. Fletcher was the Lady's family now, not MacGregor. Hoping to divert her father again, Caitrin said, "Jamie and Will and some of the other men are going to bring in the Yule log tomorrow. My ladies and I will gather greens to scent the hall with pine and fir."

"And mistletoe?"

"Aye, of course." Caitrin put a hand on his shoulder, leaned down and kissed the top of his dear head. Would her father ever recover from the darkness they'd suffered? Even though Lady Madeleine's evil son, the former Laird MacGregor, was dead by his own wicked hand these three years past, Fletcher still bore the guilt of making Caitrin known to him. She was grateful that despite the scars she bore from those awful days, they'd survived. And they'd gained a blessing in Lady Madeleine's marriage to her father. "Ye have always loved Yuletide, Da. Dinna rush past it in yer longing for spring."

He snorted and slapped the arm of his chair. "I'll enjoy it when my wife is again safely by my side."

———

THE NEXT AFTERNOON, LAUGHTER FILLED THE GREAT HALL AS Jamie, Will, and six other men struggled to carry in the massive Yule log. A phalanx of lads and the women of the clan lined their route from the keep's heavy oaken door to the hearth, where a low fire had burned to glowing coals. Fir and holly branches woven together with bright red ribbons covered the long mantle and decorated the center of the hall's trestle tables. Beribboned balls of mistletoe hung in every arch.

Fletcher stood by the keep's open door, peering out into the bailey. "Did anyone see my wife out there?" Absently, he rubbed at his leg. "I can tell there's a storm on the way."

"She'll be along later," Jamie said as he passed, hoping that was true. "Dinna drop this beast!" He admonished as one of the other men shifted his grip on the log—actually the trunk of a birch tree. "Yer toes will never be the same." He made sure his grip was firm, then glanced back to the door. Fletcher still stood vigil. Grimly, Jamie nodded to one of the lads standing nearby. "Close that or the hall will never warm." Then Jamie called for Fletcher to join them.

They reached the hearth and lowered their burden before dropping it. Still, the thud seemed to shake the very walls.

Another thud followed as the keep's heavy oaken door slammed shut. Fletcher left his post to join the men standing in front of the hearth. "Is it ready to light?"

"'Tis dry enough, " Jamie replied. "As soon as the lasses carve the last symbols, we'll be ready to push it into the hearth and for ye to put the torch to it."

"We should wait for Madeleine. Ye ken she loves the Yuletide rituals."

"We'll do as ye wish, Laird, but do ye think 'twould be better for her to come home to a warm hearth?"

"Of course. Of course. 'Tis bitter cold outside. Get on with it, lad," Fletcher agreed and waved a hand.

Jamie bent to work and kept his smile of satisfaction to himself, pleased with the number of people lingering in the hall after the midday meal. Fletcher had done just as he'd hoped and given a clear order. The longer the others in the clan saw Fletcher as still in charge and not the anxious, weakened man he was becoming, the better for all.

"My wife will be here soon and the hall must be warm and ready," Fletcher went on while he watched the preparations continue. "Has Cook made honey cakes? They're her favorites."

"Aye, Laird. I believe she has." Jamie hoped so. He gestured for the lasses to begin carving symbols sacred to the old gods and goddesses on the log. They were meant to ward away evil and bring good luck and a good harvest.

Jamie went to fetch the torch made from the remains of last year's Yule log from its place of honor under the laird's bed. By the time he returned, all was ready.

The men shoved the end of the log onto the glowing coals.

Jamie poured a cup of wine over it, careful to spread it along the part of the trunk's length within the hearth and not let it drip into the coals to flare up. As the log burned over the next dozen days, men would shove it further into the fire.

He lit the torch he'd retrieved in the embers around the log and handed it to Fletcher. "'Tis yer hall, Laird Fletcher, so yer place to bring the clan good luck in the new year."

"Aye." Fletcher took the burning torch and put flame to the log. The wine flared up immediately, then the embers around the log did, too. Once the dry wood caught fully, he laid the torch onto it and turned to face the people gathered around him. "A wee dram for all, to celebrate!"

Caitrin led a small procession of serving lasses from the kitchen, each carrying a tray of cups and a jug of good MacKyrie whisky, which they set on the tables nearest the hearth. She filled a cup for her father, then another she offered to Jamie. He accepted it with a smile, but her brows drew together. "She's still no' here." She kept her voice low. "I'm worried, Jamie. Lady Madeleine should definitely have arrived by now, even given the weather."

Jamie saw the concern in her eyes. "He keeps asking for her."

Caitrin looked toward the windows. "'Twill be dark soon. Likely her escort will make camp for the night. Should we send a rider out to meet them?"

"We dinna ken how close they might be. Lady Madeleine promised to be back for Yule. We have to believe she will. If the storm breaks tonight, a man alone will be in danger."

Caitrin nodded, but her frown deepened, her gaze on her father. "If only she were here, he would calm."

Fletcher, drink in hand, paced by a window that looked out into the bailey. "I heard something. Did anyone hear someone out there?" He rubbed at the glass. "I canna see through the fog on this pane." He tossed off his whisky and resumed staring at the window.

"I wish there was something we could do," Caitrin said.

Jamie nodded to the bottle she held. "Pour him another. Maybe that will soothe him. We dinna want him to leave the hall to wait for her outside."

Caitrin nodded and went to her father. She spoke softly to him, took his elbow, and led him to his seat by the hearth.

Jamie joined them as she added a splash of whisky to her father's cup. The log was burning merrily, throwing off enough heat to make the area near the hearth comfortable.

Cook's lasses filed out of the kitchen again, this time to set the evening meal on the tables.

Jamie took Caitrin's arm. "Shall we?" He escorted her to her place, but kept an eye on Fletcher's progress.

After they finished the meal, they again settled by the hearth, whisky to hand. The storm Fletcher predicted had arrived and was gaining strength. Rain and sleet lashed the windows.

Suddenly, the keep's door blew open with a blast of cold, damp air. Jamie hurried to close it but stopped as Lady Madeleine appeared in the doorway out of the darkness of the bailey, shaking raindrops from her cloak.

"Thank the saints, ye have returned." Jamie wrapped her in a hug, careless of her damp condition, then released her and closed the door. "We've missed ye," he told her, "more than ye ken."

"I've missed all of ye. How has he been?"

A quick glance aside showed him Fletcher dozing in his chair, no doubt succumbing to the warmth, food, and the whisky. "He'll be glad to see ye." Jamie paused and frowned. "He's had more of his lapses during yer absence."

Lady Madeleine returned his frown. "I feared that. Well, now I'm home, he'll improve. I'll see to it. We canna have him causing Caitrin to *fash*. 'Tis a happy time of year."

"Thank ye," Jamie told her softly and bent to kiss her cheek. "Ye are good for all of us, no' just the Fletcher."

"Ye are a charming man, Jamie Lathan," She patted his cheek, then stepped away and moved toward her husband.

Jamie walked with her. "Is yer escort in the stable?"

"Nay," she answered. "My MacGregor escort delivered me through the gate into the care of the stable master, and then turned for home."

Jamie frowned. "In this storm? They were welcome to stay—"

"Aye, they kenned it, but didna mind the rain. They have their own Yuletide celebrations to enjoy. Without me to care for, they'll ride fast, even if the rain turns to snow. 'Tis certainly cold enough." She shivered, then smiled. "The Yule log! How wonderful! At the door, the tables hid it from view."

Her pleasure was contagious, and her presence lifted Jamie's spirits. "Wonderful and heavy," he quipped. He beckoned the men who'd helped him carry it.

Lady Madeleine's gaze lingered on each as she thanked them. "'Twould no' be Yuletide without a great log burning in the hearth."

The men responded with smiles and nods, then scattered away.

She glanced around and nodded toward her husband. Fletcher's chin rested on his chest. "I hate to wake him." He snored, and she chuckled, then she headed for her husband. "Fletcher, I'm home! What sort of greeting is this, ye dozing before the fire?"

Fletcher spluttered awake, blinked and smiled up at his wife. "Am I dreaming?"

"Nay, husband. I've come back to ye."

Fletcher reached out and pulled her onto his lap. "'Tis about time, woman. Where have ye been?" He kissed her, then kissed her again until she melted against him.

"Gone too long, I see," she replied with a smile.

"Ye can make it up to me in our chamber," he suggested with more vigor than he'd shown in weeks.

Madeleine stood and held out her hand. "Come along, then," she said and gave him a grin.

Jamie chuckled at their antics. Despite their ages and Fletcher's infirmity, even after three years of marriage, they could still be mistaken for much younger lovers.

"Ah, praise the saints," Caitrin said, coming up behind Jamie. She wrapped a hand around his arm and leaned into him. "She's back. Da will enjoy the Yule much more with her by his side."

"Now that she's here to take some of that burden from yer shoulders, so will ye."

"He is lucky to have her affection," Caitrin added, her gaze still on the older couple as they climbed the stairs. "'Tis hard to credit her son was such a madman."

"Dinna dwell on those days. As the Lady just told me, 'tis a happy time of year. Soon enough, scents will fill the hall, from yer garlands and from the treats Cook is baking in the kitchen. We will celebrate the year past and our hopes for the future." He smiled as Caitrin's free hand settled low on her belly.

"I hope all that celebrating includes some private time of our own." Caitrin rose up on tiptoe to kiss him. "Or I'll no' be happy at all."

"Ach, lass," Jamie said, turning to wrap her in his arms, "I plan to keep ye verra, verra happy."

Caitrin rested her head on his shoulder and tunneled her fingers into his hair. "I love ye, Jamie Lathan."

"And I, ye, lass. Never ye doubt it."

She lifted her head and leaned back to meet his dark gaze. "I never will. Ye tell me every day, with yer words, yer touch, yer kiss..."

He lowered his head and took her mouth, not caring who might remain in the hall to see them. Then he swept her up into his arms and mounted the stairs, smiling as Caitrin laughed.

As they passed a window in the upper hall near their chamber, she sighed. "Ah, look! 'Tis snowing now. 'Twill be a wonderful Yule," she told him.

"Aye, 'twill. Starting now."

SEVERAL HOURS LATER, SOMEONE POUNDING ON THE DOOR OF Jamie and Caitrin's chamber roused them both.

"This canna be good," Caitrin muttered and pulled the

covers up to her chin. She wasn't one to wake up quickly—certainly not at this hour.

Jamie pulled a shirt over his head and hurried to the door. "Naught good ever came of someone pounding on the door in the middle of the night," he grumbled over his shoulder before he opened it and heard what the man who'd disturbed them had to say.

Caitrin struggled to overhear. Was her da ill? Or someone else in the keep? Ach, nay, had the Yule log sparked a blaze in the great hall? Nay, that couldn't be it. There would be more of an alarm than one man at the door. Nay, someone had arrived at the gate out of the dark and snow.

"Let them in the keep, man. Put them by the fire in the great hall. And get them a wee dram and something hot to drink," Jamie said, closed the door and turned back to her. "Lady Madeleine's escort came back, but one of their men got lost in the snowstorm. We're going to have to go search for him."

"Ach, nay." Caitrin's stomach sank. She sat up and swung her legs off the side of the bed. "Did they have any idea where they lost him?" She shook her head and sighed. "Daft question. If they did, they'd have brought him with them, aye?" She rubbed her eyes and yawned.

Jamie grinned at that. "They would." He began dressing for cold weather.

Caitrin yawned again, got up, pulled a dress over her undershift and boots over her stockinged feet. After she wrapped a shawl around her shoulders, she bent to stoke the fire while Jamie collected his weapons. "How many men are ye taking with ye?"

"Twenty Fletchers who've grown up running around the countryside. They'll ken where a man might have come to trouble."

"They will. But in the dark? In a snowstorm?"

"It canna be helped. If he's hurt, the man may freeze to death before sunrise." He went to the window and pulled aside the heavy cover. "Which should be in about six hours. On the one hand, 'tis good they didna get far in this storm. On the other, damn it, we could be searching in the dark for hours."

"Ye will take food and drink and blankets, aye?" Caitrin ordered. "I'll go rouse the kitchen while ye gather the men. Do ye think I should wake Lady Madeleine?"

"Nay, let her sleep. We'll ken more by morning. Until then, all she can do is wait and fret."

Caitrin saw the sense of that, nodded, and headed downstairs, Jamie on her heels.

The men left within minutes, the restored MacGregor men each paired with two Fletchers. Jamie believed their presence would hasten the search, as they could lead his men back to the point at which they decided to turn back and realized one of their men was missing.

Caitrin watched them ride out from the open door of the keep, her shawl pulled tight around her shoulders, but she shivered nonetheless as snowflakes swirled and danced in the frigid air. "Come back soon," she whispered as Jamie passed through the gates, then stepped back inside and pushed the heavy door shut.

She turned around with the intention of sitting by the fire to warm herself but found Lady Madeleine standing in her way.

"What happened?"

Caitrin wanted to make up a tale that had nothing to do with MacGregor men, but she couldn't do that to this woman, who had lived most of her life with men lying to her. The truth would upset her, but she deserved no less.

"Yer escort came back, but one man is lost in the storm. Jamie has taken them and twenty Fletchers out to find him."

Lady Madeleine raised a hand to her throat. "Who is lost?"

"A man named Magnus."

"Ach, nay!"

She paled so suddenly that Caitrin feared she might fall to her knees, so she grabbed her arm and put her other arm around her shoulders. "Come, let's get ye seated and ye can tell me about him."

Madeleine nodded and let Caitrin guide her to a seat near the hearth.

Caitrin sent a serving lass dozing by the fire to the kitchen for warm cider and some bread and cheese. Once the food arrived and Lady Madeleine's pallor had eased, Caitrin urged her to talk.

"Magnus, the missing man, is a favorite of mine," she related. "I met him when he was a young guardsman. He supported me while my son was still alive, at some risk to himself."

"I'm so sorry," Caitrin said when she stopped for a sip of her cider. She suspected Madeleine was being circumspect. Crossing her late son would have meant a great risk of a painful death.

"I would feel the same for any of those men who escorted me here. They all were special to me. They protected me while my son terrorized the women of the clan. Magnus was young enough at first for Alasdair to feel he could torment him with impunity, but I put my foot down and for once Alasdair obeyed me. Or if he didna, Magnus never complained to me about his treatment. At any rate, we looked out for each other, and as he got older and stronger, after he was in no more danger than any other MacGregor man, he never stopped being special to me."

Caitrin reached across and clasped her hand. "Ye ken they will find him."

"But will they find him alive?"

"It hasna been so very long. The men were dressed for the weather. I'm sure he simply got separated from yer other men. Perhaps he continued on toward home."

Madeleine nodded. "I hope ye are right, lass."

"The sun will be up in a few hours. Ye should sleep a few hours more," Caitrin suggested.

"Nay, I couldna. Ye go back to bed, lass. I'll stay here by the fire for a wee, then go help Cook in the kitchen. The lads will be hungry and cold when they return. We should have a good hot meal waiting for them."

"Ye need yer rest, Madeleine."

"So do ye, lass. I am old enough that I dinna sleep verra much, so it will do me nay harm to wait here until the rest of the keep rouses. Now go on with ye, aye?"

Caitrin went, but she knew she wouldn't sleep. Instead, she checked on her father, who hadn't roused to the commotion, then in her chamber removed her hastily donned clothes and dressed properly for the day. They would be busy, as Madeleine had said, preparing for the men's return, and there was much to do.

When she went back downstairs, she saw that Madeleine had dozed off in front of the fire. Caitrin left her there and as quietly as she could, opened the keep's door, went out into the snow-covered bailey and made her way carefully across it to the stable.

Two of the stable lads were up and already clearing stalls for the MacGregor horses. They had food and water at hand, as well as brushes and rags to rub down the horses and warm them once they arrived.

"Good lads!" Caitrin praised them. "I should have kenned ye would be making ready."

"Do ye think they'll return soon?" The younger of the lads asked, and the older one nodded his agreement with the question.

"We all hope so, aye?"

"Aye, we do," the other lad answered. "We'll have everything settled to care for their mounts when they arrive."

"Thank ye both. Should I rouse the stable master?"

"Nay, Lady Caitrin. We will be ready by the time he wakes."

"Very good, then. I'll leave ye to it."

"Do ye want us to escort ye across the bailey? It will be slippery," the younger lad offered.

"Thank ye, but ye have important work to do here. I will take care."

Caitrin left them to their work, proud that they were so conscientious. The stable master had trained them well. She would tell him later in the morning about their efforts.

By the time she made her way back into the great hall, Lady Madeleine was gone. She found her, true to her word, in the kitchen, wielding a knife, cutting up meat for a stew, from the look of the other ingredients piled on the worktable around her.

Cook nodded a greeting as Caitrin surveyed the scene. The kitchen lasses were making bread and preparing a pot of porridge. Cook was cutting up more vegetables for Madeleine's stew. They had things well in hand, so Caitrin left them to go about her normal day's duties.

Breakfast passed uneventfully, but two MacGregors arrived with a Fletcher escort soon after the midday meal. Caitrin needed only a glance to see they were exhausted and half frozen. She ordered the MacGregors to the healer for care, and took the Fletcher to her solar for his report.

"The snow is blinding, Lady Fletcher," the man told her. "Those men didna want to come in, but they were near to falling from their mounts by the time we reached the stable."

"They escorted Lady Madeleine from MacGregor, then turned immediately for home. Then rode back here and out again. No wonder they're spent. Ye havena found the missing man, then?"

He shook his head. "Nay, lady. Our lads are still trying, but may have to bring the rest of the MacGregors back here soon."

Caitrin nodded. They were all hardened warriors, but midwinter was upon them. "They'll be welcome and we'll care for them as they need." She wanted to ask about Jamie, but surely this man would mention him if there was anything she needed to know. "Very well, go get some hot food and some sleep. I hope the rest will return successfully soon, and ye willna need to go back out."

He thanked her and left her solar. She remained at her desk, deep in thought. Where along their route could a man have gotten so thoroughly lost?

———

JAMIE FOLLOWED A RIDGE THAT LED DOWN TO THE NEXT glen, cold but determined to keep going. Snow still swirled around him, all but blinding him to his surroundings. A man unfamiliar with the lay of the land might easily have confused this for the route the others took and gotten separated. But he recognized this ridge, and his mount knew it, too. They went slowly, careful of obstructions that might prove to be a hazard—or a body. Slick spots worried Jamie the most, but his horse was sure-footed and as long as they descended with care, it would keep to the track they followed.

Jamie was losing hope of finding the missing man. If he hadn't gone this way, and no one else reported finding him, he would have to assume the man had succeeded in reaching MacGregor separate from his other escorts, or else they would find his body, or what was left of it, after the snow melted.

Lady Madeleine would be devastated. So would Caitrin, for her sake, and for the man's. His loss would spoil the Yule celebration for two clans.

The track leveled off at the glen below it and Jamie paused. The man could have gone anywhere from here. Across the glen. Along it. Or he had never been here at all.

Jamie was tempted to turn back. Caitrin would be furious to hear he, too, had gotten separated from the men he was supposed to be riding with. He wasn't certain when or where exactly it had happened. He'd been so intent on the search, he hadn't noticed he was alone until he reached this ridge.

The others knew his reputation as a Lathan scout.

They were counting on him to be the one to find the missing man, and he'd let himself wander away from them. He shook his head. Go back? Or go forward?

A weak cry made the decision for him. Forward, slowly.

"Magnus!" Jamie called the man's name several times, but heard no response. Had he imagined the earlier cry? He didn't think so.

Ahead, through the swirling snow Jamie spotted a large pine. Its branches spread over a clear patch around its base, keeping the snow from reaching the ground. Was there something there? He urged his mount closer, slid off and ducked under the branches onto a carpet of needles. A man lay there, shivering, partly buried in the needles he'd clearly tried to form into a blanket.

"Magnus?" Jamie dropped to his side.

The man's eyes opened, then widened. "Ye found me. I thought I'd die here."

"Where's yer mount, man?"

"Scared off by a pack of wolves. Threw me, but the wolves chased the horse or I'd be dead now."

"Are ye hurt?"

"Aye. Leg, shoulder, wrist. Maybe more. So cold, I canna feel much."

"A blessing then. Let's get ye up and on the way back to Fletcher."

"Aye," Magnus answered, but the attempt to stand was

more than he could bear. He choked on a scream and passed out.

Magnus wasn't as heavily muscled as Jamie, nor as tall. Jamie caught him and lifted him into his arms like a child, carried him to his horse, then stopped. How would he secure the man up there? He looked around for something the horse could get close to that would allow Jamie to mount, then pull Magnus up, but the only thing he could see through the snow was the pine, and its branches draped too low to be helpful. If Magnus was conscious, perhaps he could stand and hold on to a branch long enough for Jamie to reach for him from atop his horse, but nay. No sense wasting time thinking about it, not until Magnus woke up—if he ever did.

Jamie remembered one of the Fletchers pointing out caves in the wall of the ridge he'd just come down. One he recalled had an opening that he thought his horse would fit through. The others he'd seen were too low, though they were supposed to widen past the entrance. He could carry Magnus that far, get him under cover and warm, then go for help.

Jamie trudged through the snow covered glen, leading his horse, Magnus a dead weight in his arms. "Dinna ye die on me, man. I'll nay carry ye so far to find ye gone, I willna!"

———

ANOTHER DAY HAD PASSED AND CAITRIN'S HOPE WAS FADING. The searchers had been out the entire day and returned after dark the night before but without the missing man, and worse, without Jamie. She had consoled herself that Jamie was a formidable man, and if he'd found Magnus, surely he'd sheltered with him and kept him somewhere safe overnight. She'd expected him to ride up to the Fletcher gate at any time during the day, but he hadn't.

More men had gone out before sunrise to look for him, helped by the snowstorm blowing itself out overnight. Clouds and fog persisted, but they thinned late in the day and weak midwinter sunlight pierced them in a few places.

Where was Jamie? Why wasn't he home? Yuletide was no time to be away. She wanted him here. She needed him here.

The entire clan was walking on their toes around her, and she knew it, but anxiety, nay, fear kept her short-tempered and pacing. She'd tried hiding out in her solar, but she'd felt confined in there. Yet the great hall seemed cavernous and sad, so she'd walked the bailey, even gone to the stables several times with the intent to ride out herself, but common sense held her back. There were men out looking for Jamie and the missing man. She would not add to their burdens. And the clan could not withstand the sudden loss of both her and Jamie, not with her da in his condition. They were needed here. *She* was needed here, and she needed Jamie.

Madeleine cornered her in the great hall just before

the evening meal. "Ye must calm yerself, lass. Ye are upsetting everyone else."

"How can I? Jamie is out there somewhere. He should have come back today. The storm is over. Where is he?" She wrung her hands, her distress overwhelming her, forcing her to fight back tears. "Why isna he home?"

"He will be lass. Ye must cling to that thought, as I do for Magnus's sake, and for Jamie's. They will be home. If not tonight, then tomorrow. They will arrive, or the searchers will find them and bring them home."

"Alive?" Caitrin choked on the word.

"Aye, lass. 'Tis cold outside, but 'tis naught they havena borne many times through travel and in battle. Jamie kens what to do, even if Magnus is injured."

"What if they both are?"

"Then our men will find them. Cling to that. Now calm yerself and take yer place at the head table with yer da and me."

Caitrin nodded and did as she was bid. She made it through the meal, doing her best to ignore the sympathetic glances and subdued murmur of conversation in the hall. As soon as her da stood to go, she did as well and returned to her chamber where she paced through the night, dozing only when her legs would not support her any longer.

Bright sunlight woke her. It was morning! Were they back? Or had the searchers gone out again? Why had she heard nothing in the bailey?

The faces in the great hall told her before she had to

ask. Men had gone out again. Caitrin went back upstairs and changed into riding clothes, rolled up several plaids and carried them with her down the stairs. She was headed to the kitchen to get food and cider when Madeleine intercepted her.

"Where do ye think ye are going?"

"Ye ken where I am going or ye wouldna have stopped me."

"Lass, I ken ye are worried for Jamie, and for a future without him, especially now that yer da can nay longer assume his duties as he once did. But what if Jamie returns and ye are no' here? What do ye think that will do to him? Ye must do the hardest part and wait."

"I have been waiting. I canna any longer. I must find him."

"Do ye trust yer husband? The greatest Lathan scout?"

"I do, but—"

"Nay, dinna finish that sentence. Ye trust him. Ye ken he is well and will return—with my guardsman—as soon as he can."

"I ken ye believe what ye are telling me. I want to believe it, too."

"Then do what ye can. Help yer da. Set an example for the clan that will reassure them."

Madeleine was worried for the men, too. Caitrin was being selfish, lost in her own fears and paying no attention to anyone else, or to the effect she was having on them.

"Ye are right, of course," Caitrin told her. She set aside

her plaids and went back to the kitchen to ensure plenty of food would be out soon for all of those waiting for the return of their men.

She noticed a lass in the corner by the hearth, head in her hands. As she approached, she could see the lass was crying, and closer, below the tabletop, it became clear the lass was expecting—and soon. "Dinna *fash*," she told her, putting a comforting hand on her shoulder. "What can I get for ye? Have ye broken yer fast?"

The lass lifted her head and her eyes widened. "My lady!"

"Forget that for now. Have ye eaten anything?"

The lass shook her head and Caitrin signaled to a serving lass to bring food and drink. "Ye ken I'm waiting for my husband," Caitrin told her, sitting next to her on the bench. "Who are ye waiting for?"

"My husband went out into that storm. I fear he willna come back and I will have to care for our bairn alone." She rubbed a hand over her belly.

Caitrin nodded. "We all fear for our men, but they are well used to being out in weather like this. When is yer bairn due?"

"Any day now," the lass admitted and fresh tears trailed down her cheeks. "My mother is in our croft. I came with my husband, and now I canna get back."

"The healer is here should ye have need of her. Ye will be well cared for, no matter when the men return."

"Thank ye, milady."

"Ah, here is yer food," Caitrin said as a serving lass brought a steaming bowl of parritch, some bread, cheese and an apple. "I will leave ye to enjoy it."

"Ye are kind, milady," the lass told her. "Ye have helped me to feel better."

"Then eat, lass." She stood and patted the young woman's shoulder. "I will check on ye later, but ye have only to ask anyone if ye need help."

Caitrin straightened and caught Madeleine watching her. The older woman smiled, making Caitrin feel as though she'd learned the lesson Madeleine had been trying to teach her. Caitrin nodded and moved to the next table and the next, simply talking to her people, showing them she was with them and helping where she could.

The clan could no longer count on her father. She had to be the one they could have confidence in—with or without Jamie Lathan.

———

HOURS LATER, AN EXCITED RUMBLE OF VOICES IN THE GREAT hall drew Caitrin out from the herbal where she had gone to check with the healer on the lass she'd met at the midday meal.

The door was open and people were bustling through it into the gloaming, while frigid air streamed from the bailey around them and into the keep.

Voices shouted, "They're back!"

Who was back? The searchers had come and gone several times without this level of enthusiasm. Could they have found the missing men? Jamie?

She ran past several people and slipped out the door next to another man in time to see Jamie dismount and turn to notice her.

"Get the healer!" His shout rang out and echoed off of the keep's cold stone walls.

Caitrin had never heard a sweeter sound. Her heart in her throat, she grabbed the man nearest her and sent him back inside. "Hurry!" Then she ran across the bailey and wrapped Jamie in her arms.

He caught her as she cried, "Where have ye been?" She buried her face in his neck as she clung to him, inhaling his scent and thanking the saints he was home. "Are ye well?" She loosened her hold and looked him up and down. His hair was matted and his skin reddened from the cold, but she didn't see any blood. All her fear and anxiety fled when she realized he was not injured. Exhausted, probably hungry, but unhurt.

"I'll tell all when we get inside. Magnus needs the healer. He'll be with us for weeks while he recovers." He hugged her to him and turned so they could watch the men carrying the one who must be Magnus in a sling they'd rigged from several plaids.

She and Jamie followed them inside, where the healer met them. After one look at the man they carried, she waved them toward the herbal and walked along with her patient, checking on him as they went.

Caitrin's father and Lady Madeleine joined them there while Jamie explained to the healer what he knew of the man's injuries and their cause. Hearing the litany, Caitrin marveled that Jamie had kept him alive for several days.

Her da turned to Jamie. "Well done, lad, though ye worried us all."

"I ken it, Laird, and I'm sorry for it, but I dared no' leave him, and I couldna bring him by myself without doing him more harm. We had to wait for the weather to clear for someone to see the smoke of our fire and find us."

"Dinna be sorry," Madeleine answered, stepping forward to put a grateful hand on his arm. "Ye brought him back to us."

Once the healer dismissed them, they returned to the great hall, but Laird Fletcher and Lady Madeleine continued upstairs. Caitrin and Jamie sat at a table near the hearth and signaled for food and drink. While they waited, people kept coming by to say how relieved and happy they were to have both of them back. Jamie thanked each one, giving them his complete attention until the next person approached. Finally, their food arrived and the parade ebbed.

Caitrin took Jamie's hand. "Tell me."

While they enjoyed their meal, Jamie filled her in. "He got separated from his men in the snowstorm. Wolves spooked his horse, and it threw him. Lucky for him, the wolves chased the horse."

"Maybe not so lucky for the horse," Caitrin commented wryly.

Jamie shrugged. "I found him under a pine, with all the injuries ye heard me tell the healer. He passed out when I tried to move him, which helped. I got him into a cave nearby that Fletcher men had shown me on patrol several months ago. The opening was large enough for the horse to squeeze through, too. A fire, blankets and my horse blocking the wind kept us from freezing. We ate what I had packed in the first two days. I gave him all the wine for his pain, and I hunted. That and melted snow kept us going until the men arrived. The storm kept anyone from seeing the smoke from our fire. This morning, they finally did."

"Ach, Jamie, ye must be exhausted."

"Aye, and in need of a bath." He made a show of looking around. "Perhaps I could convince one of these serving lasses to help me with that...?"

"Jamie Lathan! Ye willna." Caitrin ordered the tub and hot water to be carried to their chamber while Jamie finished eating.

ONCE JAMIE ATE, HE INSISTED ON SEEING WHAT PROGRESS the healer had made with Magnus. Her ministrations satisfied him that the man was in good hands, though he wished Aileanna were here to attend him. Magnus would be healed and on his feet in days with the Lathan healer's special talent. The Fletcher healer was doing her best, but Magnus would have a long and painful recovery.

Jamie let Caitrin usher him upstairs to their chamber and the waiting tub, steam rising from its surface beckoning to him nearly as strongly as the sight of their bed. And Caitrin.

"Lass..."

"Clean first, then we'll see about everything else, husband." She grinned to soften her words, but he had no doubt he wouldn't change her mind. She was bent on taking care of him, and relaxing in a hot tub was always high on her own list.

Still, he had to try. He wrapped a hand around the back of her neck and pulled her to him for a kiss. She clung to him, heedless now of the dirt and smoke stench of his days in the cave. Her head lifted, giving him access to her throat, telling him she wanted more. He deepened the kiss, his need for her becoming more and more heated as she gave voice to soft cries and caressed his face. He thought he might be making progress until he realized Caitrin's face was wet with tears.

"Lass!" This time, his tone was quite different from when he'd said the word only moments before. "What *fashes* ye? I'm here, safe and sound, love."

"I thought I'd lost ye," she admitted, her gaze on his chest. She lifted her reddened eyes. "All I could think of was how could I go on without ye? How could I be the clan's laird without ye at my side?"

"Ye dinna have to. I'll be by yer side."

"Ye'd best always be!"

He chuckled, but she frowned.

"I will be with ye, Caitrin. I will never willingly leave ye. Ye ken that."

"I thought I did." She set about removing his soiled clothing and tossing it aside. "I ken ye will have to go away from me at times. But I hope in those times I will ken where ye are and that ye are warm and safe."

Once he was bare, she gave him a hungry look, but pointed toward the tub. "In."

"Yes, my laird," he answered and obeyed, but a smile played around the corners of his lips. "Ye ken 'tis almost the Yule."

"Of course, I do. I've been counting the hours while ye were gone. Lady Madeleine kept me from riding out, joining the search for ye."

"Thank the saints for Lady Madeleine. I wouldna have been able to live with myself had ye disappeared." He paused and cupped her cheek. "I'm sorry I had to leave ye."

"I ken ye are, love. She reminded me, too, of what it would mean to ye if I got lost. She talked me out of going, and she was right. My place is here, helping da. And yers is here helping me."

"And the clan, lass."

"I ken it." She picked up a cloth and a bit of soap and began washing him.

Jamie leaned back in the tub with a sigh of contentment. "This is almost worth all the time I spent in that cold cave."

"Almost? What could possibly be worth more than saving poor Magnus's life?"

"This!" Jamie said and, grabbing her arms, pulled her into the tub with him.

Caitrin shrieked, but then she laughed and Jamie laughed with her.

All was well. He was home, everyone was safe, and Yuletide would proceed with relief and gratitude. And especially, with joy.

AFTERWORD

Highland history is full of battles, fascinating characters, love, hope, and tragedy. In my books, I often "set the stage" with historical events, and at times, with actual historical characters. But I also use creative license in populating my stories with fictional characters rather than historical ones, so as not to unfairly portray or impugn important historical actors.

In the series these stories come from, I have used two main historical events to set the stage.

In July of 1411, Domnhall (Donald) of the Isles and the Earl of Mar fought a battle outside Aberdeen over control of Ross territory and, according to some sources, Domnhall's plan to advance and burn Aberdeen to the ground. The battle lasted just one day. It is said that the fighting was so fierce, the ground turned red with blood, hence the name:

Red Harlaw. Overnight, Domnhall left the field and withdrew to Inverness for reasons that remain a mystery to this day. It was a terrible waste of lives, as neither side won control of Ross that day, but Aberdeen was saved. Over time, Mar succeeded in claiming the disputed territory.

In September 1513, James IV, the King of Scotland, along with most of his nobles, their sons, and many other troops, fought a battle just over the English border, compelled by the Auld Alliance, a treaty that allied Scotland with France for their mutual protection from the English. Henry VIII invaded France earlier that year, and the French king wanted James to weaken Henry by splitting his forces. For Scotland, James made a bad decision. He and most of his nobles died that day, leaving many Highland clans to be run by younger sons, and I imagine, a few daughters, as well. They spent the next several years at the mercy of the English, Lowlanders—and each other.

Find my books on Amazon in Kindle (and KU), print, and audio formats.

ALSO BY WILLA BLAIR

Highland Talents Heritage

Highland Prodigy

Highland Memories

Highland Reckoning

Highland Dreamer

Highland Echo

His Highland Heart

His Highland Rose

His Highland Heart

His Highland Love

His Highland Bride

His Highland Heart Boxed Set

Highland Talents

Heart of Stone

Highland Healer

Highland Seer

Highland Troth

The Healer's Gift

When Highland Lightning Strikes

Other Novels

Waiting for the Laird

When You Find Love

Highland Beginnings

ABOUT THE AUTHOR

Willa Blair is an award-wining Amazon and Barnes & Noble #1 bestselling author of Scottish historical, light paranormal and contemporary romance, filled with men in kilts, psi talents, and plenty of spice. Her books have won numerous accolades, including the Marlene, the Merritt, National Readers' Choice Award Finalist, Booksellers' Best Award Finalist, National Excellence in Story Telling Historical Fiction Third Place Winner, Reader's Crown finalist, InD'Tale Magazine's RONE Award Honorable Mention, and NightOwl Reviews Top Picks. She loves scouting new settings for books, and thinks being an author is the best job she's ever had.

Willa loves hearing from readers!
Contact her:
www.willablair.com
authorwillablair@gmail.com

Sign up for my Newsletter
Find links to the rest of my books